Dublin Anthology

Dublin Anthology

Sean Stones

PENDULUM PRESS

 Published by Pendulum Press
Pendulum Press, Springfield House, Bristol

CIP catalogue records of this book are available from the British Library and the National Library of Ireland.

Printed in the United Kingdom.

Paperback ISBN: 9798878571562

This book is a work of fiction. Names, characters, places, and incidents are the product of the author's imagination or are used fictitiously. Any resemblance to actual events, locales, or persons, living or dead, is entirely coincidental.

Table of Contents

Introduction

I'm not from Dublin. I'm not even Irish.

When I first came to the city, I wandered around knowing nothing about its culture or history, buying meal deals instead of chicken fillet rolls and lamenting the lack of 2-step drums in the nightclubs. I was a little English idiot, basically.

It would be nice to believe that I really became Irish, but the truth is I was always an outsider. I never saw the Cliffs of Moher, I didn't catch the leprechaun museum, I didn't even go to Copper's. I did start eating chicken fillet rolls, but still managed to pronounce 'Dáil' with about twelve syllables.

To be honest, there's only one section of the island, north and south, in which I ever felt like I knew anything — one tiny smidge. That's the walk from Mountjoy Street to Trinity College and back again: past the Dominick Street flats, onto Moore Street, through the back of the GPO, and over the O'Connell Bridge.

I did my time there: getting dirty looks from the evil bastard seagulls, smelling the chip fat on Bachelor's Walk, hearing 'cigarettes', 'tobaaaaaaaaaaaaaco' howled over and over again on grim Moore Street mornings.

It's in this bit of Dublin that these stories live. It's where Conor walks into college after his nightmare. It's where Ellie thinks on her doomed romance with Jack. It's where Salman remembers his mother freezing in the wind as they awaited immigration processing.

And the rest of it — well, I never claimed to be an authority. Actually, I don't claim to be an authority on anything.

—*Berlin, November 2023.*

Jokes

Mister Professor

Conor Crowley stumbles out of the gender-neutral bathroom and into a large lesbian standing in the doorway. Conor says sorry even though it wasn't his fault then walks back to his table. He's in a newish Dublin bar, six euro into a seven euro pint that has gone down rather more quickly than he hoped.

You can get ripped off for a pint of Guinness all over Dublin, if you know where to look. And Conor has looked longer than most. His repeated romantic failures have bestowed upon him an extensive knowledge of the city's semi-sophisticated date spots. And this bar is in the premier category.

Our handsome hero is in a bar. He is not in a pub: he is in a bar.

Dublin is known across the world for the quality of its pubs, which are imitated East and West from Shanghai to Slough. Dublin is not known – except by those who don't know the difference – for the quality of its bars.

The Dublin bar's aesthetic is far from the homely sophistication of a pub. There are no polished wood fittings, no stained-glass windows, no plump red stools. The bar is neon-lit; black walled. Motown is playing. You may order a cocktail without a fog of suspicion descending upon you.

Most importantly, though, you do not have to share the space with middle-aged men. This, rather than any gentrified aesthetic, is at the heart of the Dublin bar's appeal. And it is the reason why Conor has taken his date, Katie, here. As Conor sits down to his pint, however, he notices that a member of the middle-aged species has somehow slipped in.

To the right of the record player, just underneath the packs of wasabi peas, there is an auld fella: slumped at the bar, his mouth hanging out of a pint glass, blonde light reflecting off his wrinkled forehead.

Earlier the man was lamenting the decline in physique of modern Irish males, which he attributed to their lack of manual work and their consumption of breaded chicken rolls. This useful lecture, however, concluded as he sunk his last pint and fell into a slumber.

Katie begins to talk. Her voice is soft and earnest, and in serious moments it rises into inflection as if she is asking you to agree with her. She is dimly from the country – or, at least, Meath – but she has adopted the fashions of the city like a uniform. Leather jacket, blue boyfriend jeans, no boyfriend: no time for one, she says. And she's bisexual, she says. She just hasn't dated a girl yet.

Katie is saying something about her master's degree but, through the din of Motown, Conor can hardly hear what she says. The situation isn't helped by the laughter of some straight white males at a table near them. They're trading pointless banter and dominating their space, six of them crammed into a little booth by the bathrooms. Apart from Katie, the only women in the bar are a lesbian couple sitting inoffensively opposite the lads. Conor detected that they were lesbians when one of them kissed the other on the lips, which he tried not to find exciting or intimidating.

He looks across the table at the vodka lemonade Katie is drinking. Nearly empty. He will have to buy her another one, he thinks. Or rather, his dad will. It's Peter Crowley who covers the massive financial hole left at the end of the month by Conor's funded doctorate.

The intellectuals who run Conor's university prefer money — sorry, Business Studies — to the Arts. The fact of the matter is that a business degree is a passport to the upper middle class; and in the rough-and-tumble 21ˢᵗ century, there's not much else the university has to offer. So a giant dick of a building has just gone up to house the new Business School, the students are getting ready to learn Microsoft Excel, and the university's in the black for another year.

The downside of all this is that there's not much money for the School of English, where Conor's studying for his doctorate and trying to get a job. He ruminates on the situation as Katie talks about coming out as a vegan and her brother's academic failure. The music drowns her out.

So if I smile and it don't look dah dah dah

Conor furrows his brow, bites his lip, nods intermittently. He's not quite sure what she's saying, but he's confident he looks like he's paying attention.

It's only 'cos I'm tryna fool the something

- Are you paying attention? says Katie.
- Sorry, what?
- Your face looks weird.
- Sorry, that's how I concentrate, says Conor.

But fooling you, something, that's something something

Conor looks earnest. Katie looks worried.

- Oh. Okay, she says.

She goes on. Her brother has dropped out of college, she says.

- What was he doing?
- Business and Sociology.

Not real subjects, Conor thinks. She continues. Her brother sits at home all day playing Call of Duty. Smokes too much weed. Doesn't pay attention. Conor notices the barman waving his hand in front of the auld fella, who has fallen asleep on his pint glass. Couldn't handle his drink, Conor says to himself.

- He needs a purpose, says Katie.

Conor looks at the auld fella. He's dragging himself up the stairs, his heavy head leaning towards the floor. He doesn't look like he needs a purpose. He looks like he needs some tender loving care, and maybe a packet of crisps.

But Conor's willing to listen to Katie. He seems to believe that she possesses the same kind of feminine wisdom his mum had. The kind of wisdom that allows her to consider the world like an angel looking down from heaven.

What Conor hasn't considered that Katie might be just as lost as he is, despite being a girl.

- My dad tells him to study, but he doesn't see the point. He looks into the future and sees nothing. He needs a purpose, she says.

Ah, of course, her brother. The one who needs a job.

- Right, says Conor, he needs a purpose.

What a cliché, he thinks. Useless boy, no direction, no prospects — not until Dad steps in.

What Conor can't understand is that he's the same as Katie's little brother, just a touch more cowardly. Because instead of taking on authority aged eighteen, Conor has done exactly what his dad told him to. He's got a bachelor's degree. He's got a master's. He's got a lot of debt. Now he's doing a doctorate because he can't think of a better idea. Actually, it's only a couple of certificates that separate him from Katie's deadweight lil bro — Conor just doesn't know it yet.

- But when you ask him what his interests are, he gets defensive. I don't think he knows, she says.

Who knows? Conor thinks. Conor's interested in James Joyce, interested in detective shows, interested in the music of Billy Joel, but what kind of career does that add up to? There's this mad idea your parents push on you when you're a kid; this idea that, if you have an interest and you put time into it, someone will pay you to do it one day. But will they? Come on.

Katie finishes talking and sips the last of her vodka lemonade. Conor grits his teeth. She bought the last round; now he has to get this one.

- Want another? he asks.

- I'll get it, she says.

- Really?

- Yes, she says flatly.
- I can get it.
- What, you don't think a girl should buy her own drinks?

Actually, Conor would like girls to buy drinks more than anything in the world. Last time he was on a date his card bounced and he spent the rest of the night apologising.

- Whatever works for you, he smiles.

As she gets up to go the bar, Conor thinks about whether he should be emasculated by her gesture or just grateful. He decides he's both.

- Thanks, he calls after her.

Now a wave of anxiety crashes into him. His bladder feels suddenly full: he needs to piss, another one, the second of the date. She hasn't even gone once. He finds his balance, resets himself, breathes his anxiety out. Unfortunately, he breathes it back in again straight after.

***

Katie stands at the bar, next to where the auld fella was half asleep. They would've made a great picture, Conor thinks. A girl in the midst of life; a man in the midst of sleep — flimsy, floppy, full of alcohol. It's always that way, he thinks. He remembers his dad coming home pissed when he was a kid and his mum tucking them both into bed, father and son.

Thoughts of his mum swirl around Conor's head as he walks to the bathroom. But one half of the lesbian couple is ahead of him and – wait – she's going into the bathroom too. Great, Conor thinks, cursing the advent of gender-neutral toilets. He awkwardly catches her eye and, for a second, it looks like they might speak, until he whips out his phone and the danger evaporates. Lucky, he thinks. She might think he was looking at her just because she's a lesbian.

In the cubicle, Conor opens Gmail and prepares for the worst. He has to give a presentation in four days which will probably decide whether he is offered a postgraduate job. He's chosen to give a lecture on Irish fin-de-siecle literature, which isn't as boring as it sounds.

It's a lot more boring. Not because of the subject, but because Conor's made it as derivative as possible in an attempt to fit in with the rest of the School of English.

The ass he has to kiss belongs to Dr Gisela Guzmán, his supervisor. She's the woman who, if she has the budget, might offer him a post-grad job. The woman who will decide his fate. And look, here's an email from her now.

From **guzmangi@dub.ie**
Hi Conor,

Let's have a meeting to discuss the views within your presentation. The text may require significant alterations to its structure and perspective, and its conclusions are at times highly problematic. As I have written, this will require extensive work.

Kind regards,
Dr Guzmán
Sent from my iPad

Not great – but wait, here's another one from his dad.

From **petercrowley@uofl.uk**
Son,

Tried to call you – can't get through! How's presentation planning? You're awful niggardly taking my calls. Have you worked out what you're going to talk about? Joyce or Yeats. Not poxy Maud Gonne!!!!!!!

Dad
Dr Peter Crowley
Assistant Professor of Early Modern Literature
University of Lincoln

Conor shuts his phone off and squeals internally. Half a minute later and he's washing his hands.

- Pricks, aren't they? asks a stray voice.

The mirror shows the same eyes he awkwardly caught a minute ago: it's the girl. She looks irritated and her words are slightly alcoholic, like they've stewed in lager for half a day.

- Those lads. The way they talk about women, she says, possibly to herself.

- What were they saying? asks Conor.

- Saying how they wouldn't let a girl pay on a date, even if she wanted to. Laughing. All their little jokes.

- Oh, right, Conor nods. Is that bad?

- Yes, it's bad. Private school arseholes.

- No… I mean… letting a girl pay. Is that bad?

- Arseholes.

He leaves her muttering in the mirror as he pushes out the bathroom. On the way out, he runs into a man who looks to be setting up a stall to sell mints and deodorant.

As Conor reaches the table, Katie shakily passes him a full pint of Guinness. It's creamy and full and not something to feel worried about. Conor instantly forgets his anxiety. Assumes a calm face.

- Are you okay? asks Katie. You look anxious.

She looks anxious too. Everyone looks anxious.

- Oh, no, says Conor. This is my calm face.

One half of the lesbian couple appears through the graffiti-laden bathroom door and walks over to her table. She gestures at the lads with a hint of hostility then asks where the drinks are. Her girlfriend looks away, drunk and annoyed. Conor makes a mental note: homosexuals are unhappy too. This is somehow reassuring.

- So, you've got a presentation this week right? asks Katie. God, time flies!

Conor nods.

- I've got one too, said Katie. I'm doing it on gender and climate justice in rural Botswana.

- Oh, cool, yeah.

- For a title, I'm thinking…

She flashes her fingers across the air as if she's imagining it on the front page of *The New Yorker*.

   - 'Gender and Climate Justice in Rural Botswana.' D'you like it?

   - Yeah, sounds great.

   - Have you got a title yet?

   - Oh. I haven't completely decided yet, says Conor. Maybe 'Orientalism, Something, and Anti-Colonialism in Joyce's *Dubliners*.'

   - Wow, that's a lot of big words.

   - Thanks! says Conor.

   - So how's it going?

   - Well, he lies.

He hasn't had time to talk about all the problems with the presentation, even though they've been on three dates and knew each other beforehand. Another thing he hasn't told her is that his mum died a year ago – well, 358 days. But when would be a good time? Now?

Absolutely not, he thinks. Fuck. That.

   - So what are you gonna do next year? Katie asks. D'you think you'll get a post-doc job?

   - Well…

'Well' is the full sentence. Conor searches for an answer, or at least a way to distil 'I don't know' into something that suggests the opposite.

   - I could be an academic, he says, his voice cracking on the word 'academic.'

   - Yeah?

   - Yeah.

He pauses, gulps.

   - Didn't you say last time that you were tired of teaching English?

   - Well, he says, I… like the students and I… uh, feel I'm pretty qualified.

   - And you don't feel like you're doing it because your dad's pressuring you?

Yes.

- No. I mean, kind of. No. Can I make my answer no?

She says okay, her earnest eyes moving left to right. Her cheeks get all rosy when she's serious, Conor has noticed. He speaks.

- It is hard with Dad. He grew up in Crumlin, you know. He was poor in Dublin when being poor in Dublin was really tough. He's properly working-class.

She perks up. Conor goes on.

- But now he's an academic and he's got good money, and he did that by going to university. He went there and... turned up to all his lectures and, you know... he never left. So he kind of thinks I have to do the same or I'll end up dying in a pub, like my grandad did. He's always wanted me to go into academia.

- That's funny. I never knew your family was Irish, says Katie.

- You didn't realise I was Irish? I thought my name gave it away...

- Oh, but you're not Irish, are you? You sound so British. You *act* so British.

- Man, people are always saying that.

Conor looks sullenly into his Guinness.

- My name is *Conor Crowley*, he says.

- But you're quite...

- What?

- Sorry, I don't mean to stereotype.

- Well, my mum is from England and I grew up in Boston, but—

- Oh, cool! Boston!

- Lincolnshire. The English one.

- Oh.

- But my dad always encouraged me to be Irish, you know? He's Mister — sorry, he's a professor at Lincoln University.

- So where was the but? How come you don't think he's pressuring you?

- I don't know. I lost my train of thought.

- How come you want to be an academic? she asks.

***

The reality is this: the only thing that's got Conor this far into academia is fear of failure, and even that's been thin fuel in recent weeks.

Recently, he's tried to add a bit more postcolonial theory to his presentation in order to impress Dr Guzmán. He reads the postcolonial texts, but it turns out the words contain about twelve syllables each, and the authors seem to dislike him personally. That doesn't stop him giving his best grateful grin when Dr Guzmán mentions epistemic violence, though.

At their last meeting, he kept talking about one of the top postcolonial scholars — Edward Said — and wondering why she was looking at him with such scorn. Turns out it's pronounced 'Sayeed' — not 'Said.'

He picks up his pint, sips substantially, and opens up.

- You know, I always had this idea that I would achieve greatness. But I never worked out what that greatness would entail. I wanted to be a writer, but the trouble is that writing is so fucking boring. And so is reading.[1] I had ideas about working in TV — for the BBC, for RTÉ. But it's hard to make anything happen. It's a lot easier to scroll through YouTube.

- But you want to be an academic? Really?

- My dad is an academic. He never leaves his world. He's sitting on his arse all day telling English professors what to think about Jonathan Swift and Laurence Sterne. And nobody outside that circle will ever even bloody read what he says.

---

[1] It's true. What are you doing here? Haven't you heard of TikTok?

Her eyes focus tightly.

- Sorry, but it seems like you don't want to be an academic, she says.

- Ah, yeah. It pays decent and you get a lot of free time. It beats working for KPMG. At least I don't have to sell my soul.

Now Katie smiles a real smile. She sees something in Conor that's also in her little brother: a store of energy which, if it could just be unleashed, might become an explosion of ambition. As Katie peers into her own personal void – the one that comes after her master's – the idea of attaching herself to someone with ambition doesn't seem so bad.

It's during this tender little moment that Conor realises the lesbian couple are arguing… and it sounds interesting. He thinks he hears the word 'sex', though he's not sure. Their talk is quickly overtaken by the thump of the lads' laughter. The phrase 'unbelievable horseplay' hangs randomly in the air.

The lesbians look round. One of them – the one Conor saw in the bathroom – looks angry. The other is more docile.

- You know, says Katie, I think you and my brother might be suffering from the same thing. I feel like a lot of lads our age struggle to find a goal and focus on it.

It definitely sounded like they said 'sex'. What else could it have been?

- He did well in school – for a boy. But he never really decided what he wanted to be. I mean, it was hard for me and my sister but…

As Katie starts talking, though, Conor's ears are overpowered by the noise of the lesbians' argument. 'Sex', he thinks he hears. Surely that must be it!

- I mean he's intelligent, he's more intelligent than me…

She pauses, as if waiting for Conor to protest. But he's caught out – he has no idea what she's saying.

- Really? asks Conor, deploying his standard procedure against verbal bombardment.

- Yeah, says Katie.

There's a moment of quiet in which Katie is silent but the lesbians are in full voice, sounding like they might come to blows at any second. Added to the cocktail is the laughter of the lads, which, to the ire of the barman, is now curdling into chants about one of Dublin's most marvellous private schools.

The chants are repetitive and dull, thumping through the air like punches to the face. One of the couple looks round, clearly angry. But then she turns back to her girlfriend and, for a reason Conor can't understand, directs the anger *at her.*

Conor hears snippets of their argument. Something about 'bathroom,' something about 'women', and he's sure he hears 'sex' again. They're talking over each other and interrupting each other all at once.

It's hard for him to hear anything though. One Motown classic replaces another on the bar's record player; and between that, the chants, and the couples' argument, he can't hear anything at all. Least of all what Katie's saying.

- Really? Conor asks, unsure of what he's so interested in.

You know you make me feel like...

Out of the frazzled air Conor now snatches three words from the couple. Sex! Bathroom! Woman! As clear as day. He's absolutely sure that's what they were saying. If he can just keep listening...

- What? asks Katie.
- Really? says Conor.
- I was just—
- Really?
- Conor!
- Really?

Her gin and tonic hits his face.

Now he's listening.

- I said 'I know you don't like the comparison, but I definitely think you and my brother are suffering from the same thing.' And it's hard to grow up — I feel that too. But you weren't listening...

Shout, something baby, shout, pretty something

She inhales sharply.

- ...You haven't been listening for five minutes now. And you never listen, even when we're talking about you. You have the worst selective hearing I've ever known. You avoid any questions about your problems and you don't want to hear anyone else's. Maybe if you actually listened, you would learn something. Figure your life out, maybe.

Now she has Conor's attention. He looks like a man failing to put up a shelf.

- I'm not here to keep a little boy amused, okay? Grow up.

Shout, hooooooooooooooooooooooh, shout, hooooooooooooooooooooooooh

She slams down her glass and leaves. Conor's too shocked to say anything as she goes; but as her silhouette fades away, he notices that his initial shock has already transformed into shame. How strange. A sip of the pint will help, he thinks. He sips. It doesn't help.

Conor catches the eye of the barman, who's considering whether to go over and shut the lads up. They're in full song now, for some reason, their voices not quite drowning out the Motown. The couple, meanwhile, look so absorbed by their own argument that they're willing to ignore it all. Conor tunes in. It's the voice of the other girl, the one who was in the bathroom earlier.

- Why d'you think you're wearing a dress, then? Is that because of biology? Sex is performed.

- You're doing the same thing. It's gender that's performed.

- I know the difference. Stop patronising me — obviously I know the difference.

- I'm not — I just think you need to understand that, for some women, sex has an impact on what bathroom they want to use.

- How are you excusing them?
- I'm not. It's just—
- Then why are you on their side?

The girl from the bathroom turns round and points at the lads.

- Would you all PLEASE be quiet?

But, to her surprise, they neither cower nor attack. Instead they continue to chant.

- You're all private school arseholes, she says
- WAAAAAAAAAAAAAAAAAAAAAAAAAY, they reply in one voice. WAAAAAAAAAAAAAAAAAAAAAAAAAAAY!

It's then that Conor understands he really does have selective hearing. Bathroom. Sex. Women. It wasn't fun at all: it was just another academic conversation. He just heard the words he found interesting.

The anxiety returns, rising up his chest and rolling down his arms, which he finds he can't keep still. Out of nowhere the urge to piss returns. He downs the last of his pint and heads to the bathroom.

When he's done, he chucks a couple euro to the fella working the bathroom. The man gives him a serious look and a hand-towel.

- I'm having difficulties with girls, says Conor.
- That is normal, says the man in a Nigerian accent.

Conor wants to tell him it's more than girls causing him trouble. He wants to ask how to sort his life out. How to stop being a prick. How to grow up.

But he thinks better of it. Takes some mints. Decides not to bother him.

Lucky for the bathroom attendant, that. He's had a long day.

Chapter Two

Our handsome hero lies in the bath angrily. Ideas should be swimming around his head as the hot water soaks through his stress and washes it away. But the hot water cut out while the bath was running and, despite Conor's optimism, it's been chilly ever since.

Every moment makes the water slightly colder and slightly more unpleasant. It's those bastard flatmates again, he thinks. Using up all the bastard hot water. Doing the bastard washing up at all hours of the bastard early evening.

But maybe it's not just the water's fault. Because, as Conor sits in the cool bubbles, he's aggressively scrolling through social media.

A posh lady complaining about free school meals. A left-wing protestor getting punched in the face. A lovely picture of a tree. The posts make him sad, outraged, hopeless. And they make him want more, more, more.

As he furrows his brow ever further, an image of a child in chains turns into a vibrating black mess. Somebody's calling. Conor fumbles his phone in the bubbles and, desperately trying to dry it on the bath mat, answers the call by mistake. The voice of his dad, Peter Crowley, sounds tinnily through the speaker.

   - Conor! Finally. I've been trying to get through for days. Where have y—

     - Hi dad, just in the bath.

     - What've you got your phone in the bath for?

     - Just working on the presentation, Conor says.

     - Are you really?

Conor grits his teeth.

- Well, we're not getting hot water right now.
- Ah, Jesus. Can't you get Michael round to fix it?
Michael's his dad's little brother. Plumber.
- He's been round. The boiler's been fitted wrong.
- Jesus, says Peter. They've only fitted it – what – two
months ago?
- Three months yeah.
- Cowboys. The money they charged too.
- Yeah.
- I mean that's a disgrace, it really is.
- Well, you know, that's just Dublin.
- Not the Dublin I grew up in. My father would be
rolling in his grave. That's not how the Crowleys work.
- Well.
- And Michael couldn't fix it?
- Michael fitted it, Dad.
- Did he?
- Yeah. He's fucked it, basically.
- He has?
- But we sometimes get it on Mondays.
Conor puts his dad on speaker and sets the phone down
on the side of the bath.
- What did you wanna call about, Dad? he asks.
- Your presentation. How's it going?
- I'm surviving. I'm, uh, getting through it.
- Good. That's what counts. Get it done, and we go
from there.
Conor looks around the bathroom. Actually, his
presentation is not going well. He has written approximately
nothing and, if he wants the School of English to offer
him a job, he'll have to go from having nothing to having
something superb in… how many days?
- You've only three or so days left now, son. Best get
to it. Time flies, Peter adds.
But every time Conor opens his computer Microsoft
Word seems to spin around the screen and call him a

gobshite. So he's started to scroll social media instead. It's much better. It leaves him angry and hollow. It's much better.

The water's getting cold now. A shiver's sure to come any minute.

- Yeah, it'll be alright, Conor says.
- Good. Well. I'll keep checking in. I want to make sure you're doing the work…

Silence.

- … make sure my investment's gonna pay off, eh?

Conor tries to laugh at the joke.

- Alright then, he says.
- Alright, says Peter. You enjoy your… bath. I'll get onto Michael about the water situation.
- Alright then. Thanks.
- Bye then.
- Bye now.
- Bye.
- Bye.
- Bye bye.

Conor screws his eyes up and thinks about what Katie told him. But only for a second. Then he's back to the picture of the child in chains.

Chapter Three

Fast-forward two days. Swap the Dublin bar for the Dublin burrito place. Have you ever wondered what the spices of Mexico would taste like if they were transported to Ireland? Here's your answer: salt and rain.

Swap Katie for Oisín Mooney — a friend whom Conor met as an undergrad. Oisín's a stout lad who speaks a bit like an Irish guy doing a James Bond impression. He's done the whole private school routine: Michael's school, university, then the Dublin financial sector. He thought this might be a stepping stone to the City of London, but then, he says, 'the whole Brexit thing.'

And who'd want to go to England now, anyway? With Ireland's economy growing at 69% per year, there's more money to be made in the Celtic Phoenix than the diseased British Lion. The burritos here are more expensive than anywhere in the EU. People are drinking champagne with their 7up. Lattes are jumping around South William Street like flying fucking saucers. As Oisín's tells himself each morning, *the boom is back.*

Now he's wearing a Washington Redskins sweater, suit trousers, and a maniacal grin as he walks towards Conor's table at 100 kilometres per hour.

   - Bro, bro, bro! How's your dad?

   - Oh, alright, I guess.

   - Good to hear. We're due a real catch up. Tell me about this thing with Katie then.

   - Yeah, well it's been—

   - Oh, and really sorry I can't come to your presentation.

\- That's okay.

\- It just really got past me, bro.

\- Yeah, I know.

\- How's your supervisor as well? Still trying to save the world one citation at a time?

\- Well, you know… she just thinks the footnote system doesn't represent marginalised groups.

\- Course she doesn't.

\- How's the new girl you're seeing? asks Conor. Did you say she's a—

\- I don't have long by the way, sorry bro, so we'll have to get to it…

He glances at his watch.

\- …I can't get away from Trump Towers too long.

Trump Towers is what Oisín calls his modestly sized office block in Silicon Docks, an area of Dublin that was once a working-class suburb and had a name which is lost in the mists of time.

Our handsome hero has been feeling pretty down about the whole Katie thing. The initial shame, he found, quickly transformed itself into a richly textured nausea. To him, it tastes like nail polish swilled round the mouth.

This morning he taught a class — first year English students, dim ideas and stupid faces. He found their enthusiasm sickening, and his own pretence to be a 'teacher' even worse. The missed calls from his dad, meanwhile, have been snowballing, and he's too scared to text Katie. In fact, the only thing he's managed to do is arrange a meeting for tomorrow with his supervisor, Dr Guzmán. Now she can tell him how much she hates his presentation in person.

He's also organized a short-notice meet-up with Oisín to vent a little and maybe sort his life out. Oisín looks at him with a salesman-grin and speaks.

\- Anyway, bro, about this whole thing with Katie. It'll be grand. Sure look you're a handsome guy and you'll pick yourself up from it no problem.

- I know, man, it's just—
- Yeah, I know. But listen.

Oisín leans in like he has a terrible secret to share. Something that nobody else can hear. He looks left, right, up and down, then catches Conor's eye and whispers

- There's so many honeys, bro.

His eyes get real glazy as he says this, and Conor swears that he can see a tear welling up. Oisín seems to be looking at the honeys themselves, as if they are located in some mystical mist between their table and the soft drinks fridge.

- I know man, says Conor. But I keep fucking it up. She's so great and—
- How can you say that, bro? You're just putting this girl on a pedestal…
- Am I?
- …and you can't even look up her skirt.
- I wouldn't say that.
- Listen. You're too romantic about this whole thing. Think of girls like stocks and shares. If you go around saying your investment is fucked, it will fuck up. If you go around saying your investment is great, it will be great. The only thing that matters is confidence. With girls, it's exactly the same. It seems shite now, man, but you've gotta be optimistic. Look around you — the boom is back.

He looks at the domed ceiling of the burrito place. He seems to see it as a monument to Irish civilisation in the 21st Century. Maybe it is.

- We don't need anyone else in this country acting like it's still the fucking crash.
- But, man, she's not Tesla stock.
- No, I'd say she's worth considerably less.

His eyes zoom away for a second, distracted by a wandering ass. Then they dart back to Conor, who speaks.

- Man, I really did fuck this one up. We've been on a few dates, right? I like her a lot, man. She's clever, she's lovely. But she kept comparing me to her brother, and the whole thing was annoying me. So I kept tuning out and she noticed. She got really angry and stormed out.

Oisín gives Conor a bemused look.

- After you paid for her drink, right?

Conor thinks of how to correct the record, but before he can turn his thoughts into words Oisín breaks the silence.

- Bro, you're as clean as a whistle here. Cleaner, even. Look at it like this. She's talking about her younger brother and you're not interested. She keeps talking about it and you're still not interested. Nonetheless, she keeps talking about it. Then she finally notices that you're not interested. And for this great crime she walks out.

- But it's not just that I wasn't interested. I wasn't listening. I wasn't even trying. And I'm worried this is part of a pattern where, you know, I'm turning into this arsehole. I feel like I was doing this classic male thing: talking, talking, but never—

Oisín howls dog-like.

- Bro! You're stereotyping yourself! Look at yourself, bro. I'm sorry — okay — if a bar is loud and a person is boring, what they say will be lost in the noise. Welcome to the 21st Century. Nobody understands each other. Our generation is undersexed and overeducated.

Conor looks at the people on the table next to them. A miserable couple, both staring at their phones between sombre burrito-bites.

- I don't wanna be like that, man, says Conor. I don't want to be part of that world. It's like — I don't know man — everywhere I look, people have become retarded. Shit! I mean, not retarded. I mean…

He catches his breath just as it's about to get away from him.

- …nobody wants to learn anything anymore. None of the students can do anything but get offended. None of the old people can do anything but get outraged. None of my English tutors can even write comprehensible English. And there's so much noise: all TikTok and Twitter and nobody engaging with anything that takes longer than two minutes.[2] I don't want to be like that, and I definitely don't want my relationships to be like that.

Conor glances at the miserable couple. They're both on their phones: one of them watching a natural disaster in Asia, the other a 'top ten' video of Mexican cartel murders.

Oisín takes advantage of the moment to whip out his phone too, apologising half-heartedly as he does so.

Now Conor looks at him seriously.

- I mean it, man. It's like everybody's talking, but nobody's—

- Bro…

Oisín's shakes his head.

- …I'm sorry, but that's retarded.

He pauses a moment to let it sink in, then continues.

- You've prospects. You're on to be a big Mister Professor. You've got a huge dick right now — you just can't see it.

- It's not even about that. It's about… it wasn't just that I didn't listen to her. It's that I wasn't even trying. Man, I'm telling you: nothing makes sense right now. I want to hear what someone else has to say and actually…

He waits a second for Oisín to interrupt him. But, by some miracle, he doesn't have anything to say.

- …listen

Conor pauses for a second and lets it sink in. The catharsis. The release. The feeling of being heard. Then he notices that Oisín is on his phone.

- Oisín?

- Oh, sorry bro…

Oisín snaps it shut, revealing his lock screen: a great white shark baring teeth.

- …I hear you, he says. Your problem, I think, is this…

---

[2] Seriously, why don't you go and stimulate yourself right now? Your phone is right there.

He looks philosophical for a moment.

- …You've got too much of this political correctness stuff in your head.

Conor groans.

- Come on, man. That's not it!

- No really. I've been back at the university doing some young enterprise stuff. It's gone to shite.

- That's not it at all!

- Yeah, I'm serious Conor. Jesus, you sound like one of them. You sound like you're about to tell me how many black friends you have or something.

Conor looks equally philosophical for a moment, then sad.

- Actually, I haven't got any black friends, he says.

- Are you serious?

- Oh, no. I mean, I don't treat people differently because of race, Conor lies.

- Well aren't you a good ally. I bet you know how to use chopsticks as well, do you? You should come work in finance.

- I need a piss.

Oisín looks at Conor's burrito. It's lying there limp, losing shape as the beef bulges out of both sides. But Oisín's staring at it like he wants to make love.

- Are you gonna finish that? Oisín asks.

- You want to eat that?

- I am a weapon…

He smiles

- …of massive consumption.

- It's yours, says Conor.

***

In any case, Conor needs to piss. The urge comes with great fury, sending him into a panic as he punches his bladder and dashes down to the grotty basement toilets. An extractor fan begins to whir.

The bathroom is poorly lit and, as he unzips, he wonders if it would look any nicer if it had windows. It reminds him of a grim public toilet which he used as a kid in Boston. When he was about ten, he went in and discovered it had been lit up blue. He thought it was for Lazer Quest at the time, but actually it was to stop heroin addicts identifying their veins.

He's just ruminating on this rather tender memory when he hears frenzied footsteps descending from upstairs. This is followed by a rush at the door then a crash which shocks him and upsets his aim. He pisses a little on the floor and, red with shame, avoids looking at whoever has just entered. That is, until a firm hand clasps him on the shoulder. He spasms.

- Oh, sorry bro. Didn't mean to shock you.

Oisín. By now, the stream has entirely evaporated for Conor. He zips up and turns around.

- The hand on the shoulder is a bit much, man.

- Sorry bro. I needed to be down here, though. Not to piss, but to tell you something.

- It couldn't wait?

- I'm afraid I'm needed back at Trump Towers sooner than expected. Hold tight bro because I haven't told anyone this before.

Conor thinks about his need to piss, which has totally disappeared. He remembers how concerned his mum and dad were when he was a kid: he wasn't properly toilet-trained until age four. Back in this bathroom, Oisín looks at Conor with raised eyebrows that convey total seriousness.

- Observe my total seriousness, bro. Until now, this has not left my lips. You cannot tell a soul.

His voice bounces between the narrow walls of the bathroom. It's that weird accent again: like God tried to make an Anglo-Irish duke but switched to a regional sales manager halfway through.

- It will not leave this bathroom, says Conor.

- Good. So you know — one thing that bonds us together is the fact that we have weak bladders.

True. They met in a nightclub toilet.

- So I had to give this presentation in second year? Principles of Marketing. Pretty basic stuff by your professorial standards, bro. But it was 9AM and this was second year. I was out till closing time the night before with Steve Campbell and Dave Hevey. So this is how it happens: I get back at 3:30, skipping the afters like a good little boy. I write up my presentation that night with the aid of Red Bull and coffee.

- So you stressed your bladder?

- As you well know. So I feel like a suicide bomber with blue balls by the time it gets to morning…

A what? Conor thinks.

- …because when I explode, it's gonna be huge. But this is a presentation I cannot miss. I get to the seminar room right on time, skagged by any definition of the word. I boot up PowerPoint and immediately realise that I didn't piss before the seminar. Uh-oh.

He pauses, then goes on.

- Five minutes into the presentation and I'm darting around the room trying to incorporate punches to the bladder into my presentation style. It's a constant struggle. Agony, but I hold it. I'm just coming to the final principle of marketing — either deception or human flesh, I can't remember which — when the urge comes on like a flood. A biblical flood. So I take cover behind the lectern like it's tsunami day in Poorpeopleland and the floodgates open just as I reach my final slide. They're all clapping me as a torrent of piss is rushing down my leg. Deeply surreal.

- You mean you pissed yourself?

- Yeah.

- So what did you do?

- I did the only thing I could: pretended that nothing happened. I hid my trousers behind the lectern sure but I soldiered on regardless and answered questions as if I was right as rain. After another awkward round of applause, it was over. I got out of there as fast as I could.

- So why is this relevant?

- I'm getting to it, Conor. Restrain your big academic dick. Anyway, as I'm leaving I notice that a girl is staring at me. A really attractive girl.

- Do I know her?

- No. Laura O'Connell. American girl. Business type.

Oisín shuffles around for a second as if there's a tabloid journalist lurking round the corner. Conor wonders if it's the faulty bladder he's worried about or something much worse.

- Anyway, I'm at the door. I look back for a second, smile at Laura — totally gormlessly — and rush out of the room. Back home, clothes in the wash, and I take a shower with the image of this girl looking at my piss-stained trousers soaked into my mind. Obviously, I get drunk as soon as I'm out the shower...

The urinals flush in unison.

- ...I want to forget about it, of course. So I assemble the boys. Cans of Pratsky, a few luxury Heineken: the old Irish therapy service. And when I get to Workman's — fucked enough to forget myself — guess who comes up to say hello?

Conor stays silent.

- Laura O'Connell. She sees me ordering at the bar and says 'did you enjoy the presentation?' with a cheeky little smile. 'You're a pretty good speaker,' she says, then she bursts out laughing. Meanwhile I'm looking for a pint glass to smash my face into.

- Is that it?

- But then she says 'I thought it was great how you walked out. It was such a dumb seminar. That was hilarious.'

Oisín eyes Conor to see if he's got it. The twist.

- She never realised. She thought I was a hero.

Now Oisín sees if Conor's got the real twist. He has.

- You went home with her? After you pissed yourself in front of her?

Oisín's eyes light up and he gives a little smirk. He looks like a 70s Bond post sexual conquest.

- Got the ride too. And her sister's even nicer.

- Well congratulations mate. How is this relevant to me getting dumped?

- Can you not understand, Conor? The point is that she didn't see me piss myself. All she saw was me striding in, giving a great presentation, then walking out like I was too good for the class. Plus a cheeky smile to put the cherry on the cake.

- And so..?

- Me pissing myself was not even considered a possibility. From her angle, I really did do the coolest thing. I really was in control. So when the story is told and the facts, such as they're available, are stated plainly, the headline will be: *Oisín got the ride*. Not Oisín pissed himself. *Oisín got the ride*. Why? Because of confidence.

- I don't see how that's—

- Wake up, bro! You're the one who wants to get all philosophical about the 21st century. Here's the headline. The only thing that is important now is confidence. If you're confident, you'll get away with murder.

- Yeah, but there's a difference between you and me. You're more attractive. You always have been.

- I've always been MORE CONFIDENT. If you were more confident with Katie, there's no way she would've walked out on you. She would have second-guessed herself even if you weren't listening because confident people look like they know what they're talking about. In fact, the time to act most confident of all is when you DON'T know what you're doing. That way, no one will know you're fucking up.

He pauses for a second.

- Jesus, I'm being wise today, he says.

The extractor fan turns off and, for a moment, the bathroom is deadly silent. Oisín speaks.

   - Don't you ever wonder why everyone loves Michael Collins, but nobody knows he was armed by the Brits? Don't you ever wonder how Boris got into number 10? Don't you ask yourself what took The Donald all the way to the White House? The answer is confidence.

Oisín's own great-grandfather, Sir Charles Mooney, spent the Irish War of Independence heroically raising capital in New York for the cause. That cause was building railroad through Indian land in Arizona, but he still received a medal from the Irish Free State for his efforts.

   - Haven't you noticed that the only people who get cancelled are the people who say sorry? Think about it. The Donald. Boris. Fuck it — Kanye. The thing they have in common is that they don't give a fuck, they don't say sorry, and they back themselves. It's the people who give themselves up to the Internet Show Trial who really get their throats cut.

Oisín prepares the knockout blow.

   - There are differences between us, Conor. The first is that I'm Irish.

   - I'm Irish!

   - The second difference is that you have studied English Literature, where they teach you that the West is a corrupt, patriarchal tyranny. I, on the other hand, have studied Business, where they teach you how to make money. And there's one thing I got taught that you and all your woke friends have never got your heads round.

Now he swings.

   - Confidence is key. Now, I really have to get back to Trump Towers.

And with that, Oisín Mooney is out of the bathroom and pounding up the stairs. Before Conor can ponder the lesson of the parable, though, he hears the same footsteps pounding down the stairs. Oisín crashes into the bathroom again and says

     - Actually, bro, I need to piss first.

Chapter Four

- You've not been answering my messages all week, son, I need to talk to you! Now!

Peter Crowley's voice leaps from the phone speaker. It's thrumming and drumming and roaring with rage, but unfortunately Conor can't hear a word. It's 7 o'clock and he's ordering his second burrito of the day. The last thing he wants is a conversation.

- Listen, son, if you don't get on this quick there'll be no future for you in this profession. I'm telling you, son, we need to fucking buck up our ideas quick sharp if you've a hope of getting a job at the university!

As Conor declines extra guacamole, he hears a tinny din in his pocket. Christ, he thinks, he's left that right-wing podcast playing. The one Oisín recommended: *'EXPOSING' the Transgender Iran Lobby.'*

It's only when he pulls the phone out that he sees, to his horror, his father's name. Fuck — pocket call.

He pulls the phone to his ear and grimaces.

- Hi Dad, how are you? he asks.
- Conor? You're there.
- Sorry, I pocket called you. I'm just getting food.
- Well order something in, 'cos you've no time to cook. We need to work together on this presentation right now. No excuses, son.

The guy at the counter asks Conor what kind of salsa he wants.

- What? says Conor. Sorry Dad. I'm just getting the… the salsa. Mild, please, he says to the burrito man. Can I call you back?

- You've been ignoring my texts all day. *All week* Never mind your salad.

- I'm sorry, I've b—

- Would you give it a rest? Listen, you're not gonna like this son but…

Conor indicates his desire for sour cream to the burrito man through dramatic gesture.

- …I've been looking through your Microsoft account. I can see the work you've been doing.

- That's my account, Conor whispers furiously. Why?

He picks up the burrito. Thanks the guy at the counter. Turns around, realises he's forgotten to pay, then swivels himself back 180 degrees to tap his card.

- Because you've ignored my texts for a fucking week, Peter replies.

Conor sighs.

- And anyway, I should say the work you've *not* been doing.

- Dad, I'm trying to. I'm trying to.

- I only say this 'cos I'm worried for you, son.

- I know, dad. You've been worrying for me since I started this fucking P.H.D.

- Language!

- What?!

- Listen, says Peter, we can work through this together. I'll call you in half an hour. I can write—

- I don't want you to write it, says Conor.

- Well you don't wanna write it yourself.

- So why should I even bother?

- To get a job, why else? Listen, we'll work through it together. I'll send a temp—

- I'm sorry, dad, I'm going. I'll do it myself, sink or swim. Why bother if you're just jumping me through hoops like a fucking seal?

- A trade, for fuck's sake! Peter shouts down the line. A job!

But the line's disconnected. Conor's hung up. Not for the first time in his life, Peter Crowley is shouting at a screen.

Chapter Five

Later that evening. Another part of town. A night bright and
wild.

The cherry wood umbrella knocks into the pavement.
For each knock, four quick footsteps clack on the concrete,
producing a strange and tense drum beat.

Mr John Bonnar strides thusly towards the back gate of
the university, the wind whistling behind him and the trees
shaking like mad dogs. The full moon imposes itself on the
black sky.

Bonnar approaches the back gate, his bald head visible by
the white light of the moon. In front of him is a barrier with
cat's eyes and narrow strips of red and yellow luminescence.

On the floor behind, a pile of cracked rock. The stone
façade of a nineteenth-century gate has crumbled onto the
concrete in the high wind, leaving only rubble. A man in a
high-vis jacket hauls safety tape across it. His straining rump is
bent amongst the stone.

- Good evening, cries Bonnar.

The man in the high-vis jacket takes a moment to put
the tape down. He does so with great care and concentration,
conscious of the many steps that will need to be taken for
the gate to be restored. As he holds the crumbling stone, he
thinks of the dust that used to mark his dad's hands after a
day's work, and then — for a fraction of a moment — of
his grandad pointing proudly at the masonry on the Iveagh
Markets' walls. Then he turns around slowly to meet Bonnar's
impatient gaze.

- I'm here for an appointment, says Bonnar. With a
member of your young enterprise team.

- Sorry, you'll have to turn right for the front gate. The back gate's been damaged in the storm, the doorman replies.

- Is that so? asks Bonnar.

- It'll be closed here for weeks. The façade's come down.

- Is that so? The façade of the university — crumbling. How appropriate.

The doorman is used to these types. They come here at all hours, call for attention, then strain to make a witty remark. Academic types — all the same.

But this guy is odd even by the university's standards. He's dressed like a gentleman farmer: wax jacket, tweed cap, polished umbrella. And he enunciates every single word like somebody who's used to being listened to.

Come to think of it — he seems familiar.

- So, round the other side, eh? asks Bonnar.

- Yeah, just turn right and you can't miss—

- Good man.

He turns to leave. As he does, though, the doorman stops him.

- Sorry pal, do I know you from somewhere? The telly or—

Bonnar's eyes twinkle through the dark like fireworks.

- You may do, he says excitedly. Do you watch our videos? Or our podcast?

- No, nothing like that. Nothing recent. Were you on… something in the 2000s?

Bonnar's eyes switch instantaneously from excitement to irritation. So he hasn't seen him recently? Where has he been — under a rock?

Bonnar has been in this situation many times before. The person always stares gormlessly in the air for a few moments before – eureka! – he remembers that infernal detective drama. And here it is: the doorman's smile curling with joy as he rekindles his pathetic enjoyment of that low-grade ITV police procedural.

- Aaaaah! Falmouth Smart…

Yes, yes, the name of the detective.

- *True Kent Detective!* We used to love it. Case closed!

Yes, the bloody catchphrase, as if the dolt doesn't realise he hears it every day.

- Yes, well thank you for your appreciation, says Bonnar.

- That's fantastic. Are they bringing back the show anytime soon?

- Not likely. I don't act now. I broadcast.

- That's a shame.

- Is it really?

- Ah, it was a great little show. Case closed!

- Well I'm not so bloody sure… The last thing I want is to be back on that pitiful detective show gawking around rural courts like a bloody National Trust employee. I'm a broadcaster now. So, if you don't mind, I'll be on my way. You might not know it, but this university has more to worry about than a fallen façade — appropriate metaphor though that may be!

Bonnar scuttles away into the night, his Oxford shoes clicking and clacking against the concrete.

Meanwhile, the doorman watches in silent rumination. The fella's turned left, not right like he told him to. He supposes that's just academic types. Detective Falmouth Smart of the Kent Police would never make a fool of himself like that.

***

The lights have gone out over the staircase. Bonnar soars up them, his footsteps pounding on the well-worn stone even though he can barely see. Late. But not his fault, he thinks — that remedial workman pointed him the wrong way. Bonnar's heading to the oldest part of the university, to a room first used by the univeristy fencing club in 1756. Now it's in the hands of the young enterprise society.

Bonnar, ten minutes late, opens the door and steps in with the cold. Waiting for him is a warm schoolboy face — Oisín Mooney. He leans happily on a chair tucked into a table.

- Case closed! says Oisín. Mr Bonnar, let me just say I'm a huge fan.

Oisín Mooney stretches out a hand. Bonnar winces.

- Very good, says Bonnar. Now, to business.

- Oh yeah, says Oisín in a silly voice.

Bonnar frowns, then lays some papers on the table behind Oisín. Oisín has to bumble around to see them.

- A matter of extreme importance has been raised, says Bonnar. As our man in Dublin, your task will be to aid me in this matter — to its conclusion. There is a long operation to come. Much pain will be endured. But if we pull this off, we won't just be getting attention here. We'll be getting coverage across the UK, across the United States, across *the world*

- What is it? Oisín asks.

The wind batters the walls.

- There is a long journey to come. I hope we can trust you to be with us all the way. Because, if you are, you will find yourself exposing the most shocking crime ever perpetrated at this university. A crime so sour and gross that it exposes corruption at the heart of *all* our academic institutions.

- What is it? Oisín repeats.

He really does look like Falmouth Smart, Oisín thinks. Just the picture of the no-nonsense Kent detective. And these monologues — they're exactly like they were at the end of each episode. Oisín's practically waiting for him to point a justice-loving finger and shout 'case closed!'

- I have no hesitation in saying this, Oisín. If you choose to accept this task, you may find yourself in a position to help with the expansion of our media organization. You may find yourself with a massively enhanced profile. You may find your reputation attacked, yet, in the eyes of the courageous, you may find yourself…

The full moon glows yellow behind Bonnar's wide eyes.

- …a hero!

Bonnar looks out the window messianically.

- What is it? asks Oisín a third time.

Bonnar pulls his gaze from the window and looks at Oisín in irritation.

- Well look at the paper! It's on the table, he says with exasperation.

Oisín reads it. Whooshes his eyes over the text. Lets his jaw drop.

Then he sees it. Amidst the shocking revelations, the hideous facts — amidst them, a name. And not just any name.

- Hold on, he says to Bonnar. That's…. that's…

Bonnar's mouth opens.

- …That's Conor's supervisor!

Chapter Six

'Before the woke activists engulf us in an identitarian dystopia, some low-level civil war, which already has been breaking out in America, we must act. You can wait, and you can try to appease the mob, and can hope that the mob will pass you by...'

Conor trips along the cobblestones of the university, a bitter March wind on his face and a podcast recommended by Oisín in his ears. He's on his way to teach the dreariest class he has: a group of second years who, with one exception, keep a conspiracy of silence every single week.

'...But they will not, whether you work in a university or not. Make no mistake. This overreach, if it is not stopped, will lead us into a dystopia from which we may never escape: the end of Western civilisation. And now a message from our commercial supporter Vitrant, whose refreshing drink mixers hydrate you quickly! We all know how important vitamins are – to regulate body temperature, to keep joints lubricated, and to aid memory. But, with so many supplements out there, sometimes it's hard to know exactly what you're getting. That's why I use Vitrant drink mixers, which have all the vitamins you need for the day in one refreshing mix. My favourite flavour is grapefruit but the other flavours are just as tasty! Plus they're great for those little monsters, whatever their ages! I'm John Bonnar. Try Vitrant today! Free delivery across the UK!'

Conor enters the Arts Building and wonders at once whether he's getting enough vitamins.

He buys multivitamins, but only the Aldi ones — they don't sound as good as Vitrant. And walking through college this morning, he did see that some speaker at the college had been deplatformed. Everyone's getting cancelled these days.

But it sounded like the speaker had some reasonably dodgy views and he's not sure about this podcast which Oisín recommended to him anyway. He's definitely not sure about ordering special vitamins from Britain when he's already blowing so much cash on pints and burritos.

Maybe that's not because of the podcast. He's just come from a meeting with his supervisor, Dr Guzmán, which has left him feeling confused and childish. What he understood was that his presentation is shite. And he's almost certain that Dr Guzmán won't recommend him for a post-doc job when he finishes, even if he does everything she asks.

Now his phone beeps at him. It's his dad, texting a friendly reminder.

STOP ACTING LIKE A CHILD. YOU ONLY HAVE A DAY LEFT, SON. CALL ME URGENTLY.

He checks for the text he really wants. Katie. She still hasn't sent a word. He looks at the Notes on his phone, where he's drafted thirteen apologies to her and sent none. Sighs. Enters the seminar room. Throws his phone across the table.

He takes a scrunched-up manuscript out of his bag and throws it on the table too. The notes for his presentation.

It seems that Dr Guzmán's comments on his draft are not just difficult but literally meaningless. He stares at the text as the words blur together, then float around the page individually like wisps of smoke. Conor wonders if he's going mad. Then it occurs to him that he might just be stupid.

***

The meeting with Dr Guzmán had been a disaster. Conor knocked on the open door of her office, projecting a cool, casual air, and said with a cheeky smile

- Hi Gisela. How are you?

- Call me Dr Guzmán, not Gisela, she replied without a cheeky smile.

She closed a book which was sitting on her desk. She was wearing a bright dress with African-inspired prints and large hoop earrings.

- Oh, right, sorry, said Conor.

- So, your presentation? Dr Guzmán asked in her American accent.

- Oh right, it's 'Joyce's *Dubliners*: Orientalism, Anti-Colonialism, and…

He searched for a third. You always have to have a third one: that's how titles work. His eyes turned to a brass name plate on the desk.

Dr Gisela Guzmán

Reader in English Literature

- …and English Literature, said Conor.

- Why English Literature?

- Well, he said. I… can change it.

And it just got worse from there. Dr Guzmán didn't seem to like him — which Conor nowadays thinks it pretty reasonable. But he usually shrinks into himself when people don't like him and he's always found that this defuses the tension superbly. His mum was the only person who didn't buy it.

It doesn't seem to work with Dr Guzmán, though, and Conor can't figure out why. It might be because he finds her so attractive — her semi-street-smart tone, her dark features, the hint of awkwardness beneath her self-assured exterior. But he suspects it's much simpler than that.

Actually, it's probably down to a simple communication problem. Most of the time, Conor literally can't understand what Dr Guzmán is saying.

- It's very important that you familiarize yourself with the scholarship on cultural appropriation. Copy it all if you have to. Take this argument by Eric Lott. Lott's been a very important influence on me, with the emphasis he places on

performativity and deconstruction. Have you read any of
his work?

- Yes, of course, Conor lied.

There was an irresistible hunger in Dr Guzmán's eyes.
She looked like a priest who, having received confession,
had decided to go for a cheeky exorcism. Conor nodded as
she reached into her drawer and snatched a well-annotated
hardback from within.

- Ah, here it is. He's analysing a song from the
nineteenth century here. Blackface minstrelsy.

'But den one night he danced high,
He run his heel in a black gal's eye—'

She raised herself from her chair and, with no discernible
hesitation, performed the song herself. Her feet stomped in
time, shaking the office walls, sounding half Louis Armstrong
and half Chewbacca. Conor looked on breathless.

'Oh! Golly me, but didn't she cry!
Unlucky Old Blind Josey.'

- Innocent enough, right? She said as she sat back
down.

A forced smile beat an awkward track on Conor's face.

- I'll quote directly from Lott's analysis, said Dr
Guzmán...

'...On the most immediate level, collective white male
violence toward black women in minstrelsy not only tamed
an evidently too-powerful object of interest, but contributed
to a masculinist enforcement of white male power over
the black men to whom the women were supposed to have
'belonged'. Indeed the recurrence of this primal scene, in
which beheeled black men blind black women, certainly

attests to the power of the black penis in American psychic life…'[3]

...Brilliant, right? she said.

- Oh. Yeah, said Conor. I'd, um… never thought about the power of the… you know. I'm sorry. Did you say penis?

- Right, she smiled. Penis.

He swallowed vociferously as she sat back down. Then she gave a shy smile as if she'd received top marks on her homework. It was like a little girl was in the room — if only for a slim moment — before the Reader in English Literature returned wearing her most serious face.

- Yes, Lott's very good on this. This kind of powerful, almost *sexual*, attraction to other cultures that expresses itself in appropriation, in *copying*. On the fetishisation therein but also the love. The genuine *love* for black music these blackface performers feel, in all their damaged colonial mentalités. It's startling. As Afro-Latina myself, I'm thinking about how African musicians have been pushed to the margins. I'm thinking about my ancestor's role in this music. I'm thinking about…

Conor nodded enthusiastically, trying to hide his confusion. As she began a lecture on the history of black music, he couldn't help but feel slightly ashamed. He didn't know the names of the groups. Actually, he only really listens to Billy Joel, Les Misérables, and Maxwell's Silver Hammer by The Beatles. But even that he hasn't heard for a while.

- …and this goes all the way to the footnote system. I mean, I've done a lot on systematic discrimination in our footnote system. On the way it sends scholars of colour to the margins...

As she concluded her lecture, she laid her hand softly on the desk and caught him dead in the eye. Then in an instant her stare was gone and her eyes were darting scattily about the

---

[3] Eric Lott, 'Love and Theft: The Racial Unconscious of Blackface Minstrelsy', Representations, Summer, 1992, No. 39 (Summer, 1992), pp. 23-50.

room. Conor felt heat in his body and looked away from her to try to cool it.

What he saw was walls without windows, peppered with pictures of Angela Davis and Malcolm X. They looked like teenager's posters of favourite pop idols, only they were weirdly blended in with paintings of medieval jousts and monarchs and… was that Edward of England, the Black Prince?

- Well, she smiled, this is exactly the kind of thing you need to get into your essay.

- That's, uh, interesting, but… I mean my essay is about 20th Century Irish Literature.

- And you don't have much time. You've only got a couple of days. *Dios Mio.* Time flies!

- Thank you but, do you think… how can I apply that to 20th Century Irish Literature?

- I can't do your work for you Conor, she smiles. *¡Qué Lastima!*

There was a pregnant pause. Then Conor said

- D'you think I need to look more at the, uh, colonial disc—

- That's exactly right. What you need to do is look at the colonial discourses at play here. *Dubliners*, for example. There's a story called *Araby*. As in 'Arabs.' *¡Mamma Mia!* Think of all the colonial structures that underpin this…

Her raised voice got stuck in his ears.

- … And how does the fact that you're a white male impact your study?

- I guess, uh, I was planning to take a more objective approach.

- Objective! Objective! *Qué Sorpresa.* White men have been 'objective' for four hundred years, and where has 'being objective' got us? Have you been watching the news?

- Um—

- *Qué Sorpresa* means what a surprise, by the way.

Then she handed him a thick book with her name on it.

- This is what I was working on the last… three, four years. Well, it's my life's work really.

White Jousts, Black Helmets: Blackface Minstrelsy and the American Appropriation of Medieval Jousting 1777-2020
By Dr Gisela Guzmán

- I was very lucky, she said. One journal called it an 'effortless application of Critical Race Theory to the cultural politics of medieval jousting.'

He flicked through it; found the final chapter: *Wherefore art thou my N——!: Hip-Hop Resistance, (In)Docile Bodies, and the Neoliberal (Un)Record Industry 1989-2020.*

Dr Guzmán looked proud. Conor looked confused.

- Uh, I can see what you're getting at, Gise— I mean Dr Guzmán. But, and I know I should get this, it's just I don't really know what 'neoliberal' means. I mean I know what it means, of course, it's just… in this context, you know?

She smiled. He could see how much she enjoyed these moments, these true moments of instruction, where she could truly and sincerely see her students growing not just as scholars but as human beings.

- Come on, Conor. Look around you. *That's* what neoliberal means.

Conor looked around the room. A small desk, a Starbucks coffee cup, a wi-fi extender which didn't seem to work. It was hard to pinpoint exactly what was neoliberal about it.

- Right, but I mean, if I'm, uh, to use these, I might need something a bit more precise.

- What you need to understand is that these theories apply to *everything*. That's what's so exciting about them — you can't avoid them — they're *everything*. The intersection of race, gender, and sexuality — it's *everywhere*. Literature, music…

She looked longingly to the picture of the Black Prince on the wall.

    - … jousting.

Her gaze fell upon her book with religious reverence. Conor again read the title: *White Jousts, Black Helmets.*

    - Once you know Social Justice, once you really know these theories… you will see them everywhere. Everywhere, she repeated. *You won't be able to stop seeing them*, she said. But you have to believe, Conor. *You have to believe.*

Conor said thank you and left promptly, having found himself struck with a sudden need to piss.

***

Now our handsome hero sits in another windowless seminar room. He's preparing notes for the class he'll teach in a moment. Second years: *British and Irish Children's Fiction* is the module name. The title is 'Harry Potter and the English Schoolboy Novel.' Supplementary reading: a chapter from *Tom Brown's Schooldays* which he picked at random and an academic article which he picked because he actually understood the introduction.

He touches his face, red from the room's stuffy heat. He is sitting at a desk rigorously re-reading his notes.

Or he should be. Actually, his eyes meander between Facebook and old messages from Katie. He hunches over his laptop, the ceiling fan above him creaking occasionally and generally giving the impression that it's not keen to stay on the ceiling.

He wonders whether there's asbestos in the room above him: some workmen found it in the building a couple of weeks ago, he heard. The budget of the School of English has been frozen since the university overspent on the new Business School, though, and he's sure that the department doesn't have the spare money to both employ him and remove every last bit of asbestos.

He loses his wi-fi connection and his Facebook page freezes. Fine God, he thinks, I'll look at Dr Guzmán's comments. He turns to the scrunched-up manuscript on the desk. To her comments.

You should 'sufficiently account' for your positionality rather than overcome it?

He tries hard to focus, taking each word one-by-one. Positionality. That's the political position from which you write, right? But why did she use a question mark?

This is not discursive analysis. Use of heuristic approach.

Discursive is like discourse. Talking. Heuristics is like… trying to make theory work without theory. Or…? That's…

He notices a buzz in his ear and looks around to see where it's coming from. Nothing. *Positionality.* He shakes his head to try to bring his eyes back to the words on the page. *Positionality.* Buzz. Louder. The beeps of heart monitors. He suddenly feels sleepy. *Positionality.* He loses focus on the page as the word *positionality* floats around his peripheral vision.

Every time he thinks he has brought 'positionality' back into focus it splits into two and each fragment drifts away. He shakes his head again — violently — and *positionality* comes back into focus, only to splinter into bits and drift around the room. The *pos* is suspended in the light above him. The *ality* is very hot all of a sudden. Buzz. Louder. A woman in a hospital bed. He closes his eyes.

Positionality

It appears on the screen of his closed eyes. As if he cannot escape it even when he can no longer see it. Buzz. Louder than ever. Positionality. His head hits the table.

His head stays on the table.

***

Conor is unconscious at his desk, half dreaming about his mother.

- Dr Crowley? Dr Crowley?

A rapturous knock at the door.

- Fucking hell, Conor grunts to himself.

In the glass of the door, he sees a pale girl looking down on him. Between him and her hangs harsh white light from a strip lamp. As Conor squints, it projects an artificial halo behind her head. When he catches her eye, though, he sees that she is looking at him with disgust.

- Oh sorry Samantha, come in, he says.

It's Samantha Kunz-O'Connell, a second year from Massachusetts. She is wrapped in a sloganed t-shirt and a tote bag which advertises her hostility to animal testing. As she walks in, Conor reflects on how little he cares about animal testing.

- Hi, Dr Crowley, I was wondering if I could talk to you before class? I prefer Sam, by the way, she says Americanly.

- Of course, what can I help you with?

- Well, Doctor, I—

- You don't have to call me Doctor, Sam…

But I love it when you do.

- … I don't have a P.H.D. yet.

Maybe he should've lied, he thinks, shrugged his shoulders and accepted the compliment. That's what Oisín would've done.

- I need to talk to you about decolonising children's fiction, she says. My last essay. I think you made some, um, unfair criticisms, and that was reflected in the mark.

You mean 'diversity in children's fiction,' Conor thinks — but doesn't say. That was the name of the class.

He throws his mind back to the essay in question. It was good, he remembers, but a bit overzealous. There was no counter argument at all. She got a high 2:1, though: not bad; not brilliant either.

- You got a high 2:1, says Conor. That's brilliant.

- Well, the mark isn't really important. It's the criticism you gave me.

- You can sit down by the way.

- No, that's okay. I'll stand.

She shuffles around in front of him as he tenses up in his chair.

- Well, the only criticism I remember making is that the essay lacked a developed counter argument. That, he says, is something you need to work on, but the essay as a whole was very goo—

- Yeah, that's what I mean!

She reddens. From nowhere, it looks as though she might break into a million pieces. She slams her phone on the table.

- I think it's unfair to ask for a counter argument when this is such an important topic. We're talking about a colonised space, right? This is about standing up for what's right, and it kind of sucks that you want me to... defend the lack of representation here. I think the way you're framing it is problematic. Like I'm not going to accept a counter-argument — even if I have to sacrifice my marks. I'm not offended...

She's definitely offended, Conor thinks.

- ... but only a tiny minority of children's literature has LGBTQ+ characters and even less has children of colour, says Sam.

Children of colour? When did that one slip in? Conor asks himself. Who are these colourful children?

- I'm, uh, sorry Sam. What in particular did you disagree with?

- I didn't disagree with it. It's problematic. The question is 'Assess arguments about representation in British and Irish children's literature.' So there aren't enough children's stories with female characters, or characters from any other minority, right? You can't expect me to say that everything is fine, and that there shouldn't be any change?

As she stands above him, Conor thinks about what 'problematic' means. He hears it all the time: when shows from the 90s are on TV, when the word 'homeless' is used, when Tesco sells a jerk chicken wrap. But what actually is it? He asks himself. Like, apart from a synonym for 'bad.'

- I mean, I'm in a position of privilege right. I completely recognise my privilege as a white woman, and that's why it's so problematic. I mean I'm Irish so I'm not, like, as white as someone like you, but I still—

- I'm Irish! My dad was born in Crumlin, says Conor.

- Where's Crumlin?

Why does no-one ever let me be Irish? Conor thinks. He's sick of these Irish Americans holding a monopoly on the diaspora. Why does everyone think that the Irish go to England and immediately join the Conservative Party?

Sam, meanwhile, looks at him with disbelief.

- Really? You just seem so British.

- No — I'm — no. I mean I *am* English. I grew up there. But, I mean, it doesn't… what were you saying?

- As a white person I benefit from this oppressive system. If I argue that the colonisation of children's literature should be maintained, I enable that oppression, right? Like if I make a counter argument that could be an act of verbal violence against people of colour.

- I mean, yeah. Okay. And you don't think that there's a counter argument to that? Like. Maybe some, uh, people of colour might disagree with you?

- Of course. People of colour vote against their interests all the time. People of colour *think* against their interests all the time. They can be so disappointing. And as a white person, there's certain parts of the oppression I can just never understand.

Okay, thinks Conor, tuning out. That's what it's about — she doesn't understand. He congratulates himself. With this next sentence, he thinks, he'll fix the whole thing.

- That's absolutely okay, Sam. Nothing to worry about. So what was it that you didn't understand?

- No!... You don't get it...

Oh.

- ...I understand that I don't understand. In order to be an ally, you first have to understand that you can never understand what it means to be... to be a person of colour.

- But if you don't understand, how can you make an argument at all?

- By allowing them to speak, and checking my own privilege. By understanding that I CAN NEVER UNDERSTAND.

- I'm sorry, says Conor weakly. I don't understand. I mean… I'm not quite sure what you're getting at. Understand what?

- Their oppression.

- Who?

- People of colour.

- Where?

- Here.

- Here?

Conor looks into the corridor.

- Everywhere. Throughout Western society. In the colonial architecture of the West. Colonisation. I will *not* support it in my essay. And *you* should stop sustaining it by telling us to argue like *colonizers*.

It all makes inarguable sense — like a huge boulder rolling down a hill. Conor's brain shivers.

Sam, meanwhile, casts her noble gaze up at the ceiling fan. He looks over her essay again. Finds a passage halfway through:

A writer of Whiteness or any other hegemonic discourse must represent their opinions within that discourse. Any other approach risks further disempowering already disempowered groups, which constitutes verbal violence and contributes to physical oppression.

He looks up at Sam, who is looking down at him with something in her eyes between sadness and disgust.

- Uh, I, uh, see what you, uh… I think I'm beginning to get what you're s—

- It's obvious, Conor. It's your positionality. That's the problem.

***

It's at this point that Conor sees several skittish faces looking at him from the corridor. His students!

He looks at his phone. It's ten minutes after class was supposed to start. Thank God.

- I'm sorry Sam, we'll have to do this after class. Sorry, everyone! Come in! Come in!

A disappointed look appears on their faces as they realise that class isn't cancelled after all. They each wrap up their work on TikTok and Instagram, then take several hours to sit down. Conor smiles giddily as he realises that he doesn't have to talk to Sam. Not directly, at least.

He puts his teacher's voice on.

- So, how did everyone find the reading?

Purgatorial silence greets him. It goes on, and on, and on, until Conor detects that he is losing the room. A girl in the corner has clandestinely opened up Instagram and one of the boys is watching an ISIS beheading.

- Perhaps that question is a bit broad. Today's class is on Harry Potter. How many of you have read Harry Potter? Or seen the films? he adds, casting a net as wide as the ocean.

Pale arms snake to the ceiling: a few students putting their hands up.

- So, two questions. And the controversy comes later. What did you think of it when you first read it? And what do you think of it now?

Silence in the room. A few throats are cleared, as if something might be said, but silence returns instead. Conor clears his throat as well, hoping that it might spark some ideas. It doesn't spark any ideas.

This, Conor thinks, is the paradox of the 21st century university. You've read the right-wing press. If you've a traditional mind, you'll think that students spend their seminars plotting to take down statues of Sir Winston Churchill and gasping in horror when someone mentions the United States of America without a trigger warning. If you've read a Sally Rooney book, you'll think they discuss their feelings and wear nice woolly jumpers and have sex with each other when they're not too sad.

But that's just it. It's not like that at all. It's not *1984*. It's not a marketplace of ideas. It's just…

Conor looks around the room. Blank eyes, bored lips.

He sighs. These kids don't need to shut up, he thinks. They need to speak up. They don't need to learn respect, they need to learn how to string a sentence together. Anything to break the encroaching silence.

They're not snowflakes because, although snowflakes are fragile, at least they actually exist. They're software. Take them off their devices and they vanish into thin air. Presumably they have an interior life; it's just impossible to detect, like a subatomic particle or a gay football player.

Nobody has any opinions on Harry Potter. Well… they might. But, if they do, they don't want to let them out into the world.

Maybe it's the constant judgement young people face, Conor thinks. They *are* the first generation in history that can't even share a beach photo without being greeted by a precise numerical measurement of how many people like their tits.

- Do ANY of you have ANY opinions on Harry Potter? Or J.K. Rowling?

A look of excitement comes onto the face of one of the boys, and for a moment Conor thinks he's going to speak, but it turns out that's he's just got to an interesting part of the ISIS beheading.

Then there is a sign of life. Conor is greeted by a sound like a yoga mat scraping concrete. Sam clearing her throat.

- Actually, I think J.K. Rowling is quite problematic.

***

Thirty minutes of silence follow punctuated by occasional murmurs of agreement. All the students seem to agree with each other, which is great for them because it means that they don't have to debate anything. After several awkward silences, Conor cuts the seminar short.

The students scuttle away like priests from a brothel. All except Sam.

- So, says Conor, you want to keep talking about the, uh, essay… well, if you'd like to see me sometime this week that would be great. Great contribution today, by the w—

- Can we talk about it now?

Fuck! Thinks Conor.

- Certainly! says Conor. It's just that, uh…

Conor searches his brain for an excuse but all that flashes up is

Positionality

- Uhhhhhhhhhhhhhhhhhhhhhh…

Just as his 'uh…' is becoming impossible to sustain, though, he is saved.

His phone buzzes in his pocket. Somebody is ringing him. Fucking yes! He thinks. He takes it out of his pocket. It's his dad, on WhatsApp. Fuck no! He thinks. Still, Sam will have to leave if he answers.

- Sorry, Sam. I have to take this. Email this week. Or, if you really need to, wait outside.

- I'll wait outside, she says.

- Great, see you later this week then.

As Sam picks up her tote bag, Conor inhales deeply. Picks up the phone.

   - Conor, what the hell is going on? You've barely a day left till the poxy presentation and you're still ignoring me? What's going on? I can't let you mess this up! D'you want to get your P.H.D. at all?

No, thinks Conor.

   - Yes, of course I do. I just—

   - Well, why aren't you acting like it? You're about to run out of time. D'ye not fucking understand that?

It's a funny thing that Peter Crowley does when he's angry. Drops his English critic voice and starts speaking like Conor McGregor's grandad. Conor's not sure which version of his father is the real Peter Crowley and he suspects that Peter might not know either.

Conor clutches the phone close to his face. Sam is still packing her stuff up and she's taking an unprecedented interest in the organisation of her bag. He's sure that she's listening in: her ears pricked up when his dad swore a moment ago.

   - I know, I know. It's hard, Conor whispers into his phone.

   - Well d'you have to be such a girl about it? I'm on your side, son, I really am. Just be straight with me.

Conor stifles a gasp at the sexist language, then looks around to see if Sam heard. Through her innocent smile, he thinks he can detect a judgmental look. He's got to defuse the situation.

   - Yeah, terrific, Conor says. Just fantastic.

If he can just adopt a jovial tone, Conor thinks, maybe Sam will believe that he's shooting the breeze with an old pal in the Home Counties. Then, when she leaves, he can really get angry.

   - What? What the bollocks are you talking about?

   - Is that right? Henley-on-Thames? No, no, more for the cricket. Thank God.

\- What are you talking about?

Finally, Sam seems ready to leave, or at least to have lost interest. She canters out the door at last.

\- Bye Samantha!

The door shuts and Conor turns from Young Conservative to rabid dog.

\- Dad, for fuck's sake, you can't say 'act like a girl' anymore. You're an academic — how d'you not know this stuff?

Mostly, he's annoyed that his dad called him a girl. But he adds in a dollop of self-righteousness because of the language.

\- Jeeeesus, don't talk to me about being an academic. Look at the state of you. If you don't pull your finger out, you'll be lucky to get a job pulling pints, never mind academia. Well that's grand!

\- Jesus Christ, why do you have to assume that it's going badly?

\- Because you're being niggardly with the truth. If it's all grand, why haven't you picked my calls up in a week?

Conor clasps the phone tightly.

\- Christ Dad! You can't say that any more.

\- What are you saying? 'Niggardly'? It's nothing to do with colour — it's very common in Early Modern English. Now stop fucking changing the subject!

\- Dad, *please* don't fucking say niggardly!

\- Stop changing the subject! I can't let you fuck this up, son. I need to make sure you're alright!

Suddenly, the room is very hot again. Conor's face is full of blood.

\- So what if I fuck it up?! At least it will be my own fuck up, not yours. At least I'll be drawing out my own life, not colouring in yours! I don't want to be an academic!

As Conor says this, though, the wi-fi connection drops for a second. This causes Peter to miss most of what Conor has said.

The angers comes through, sure. But Conor's confession that he doesn't want to be an academic goes missing somewhere over the Irish Sea. Peter therefore assumes — fairly, it must be said — that Conor is still lecturing him on political correctness. Which is a shame.

- COLOURED? WHAT THE BOLLOCKS ARE YOU TALKING ABOUT COLOURED PEOPLE FOR?!

Unfortunately, the Crowleys have never been expert at emotional expression; not least since Conor's mother died. Since then, it's fair to say that their skills haven't improved.

- WILL SOMEONE LET ME FINISH ONE BLOODY SENTENCE? says Conor. I DON'T WANT TO DO THIS. NOT COLOUR. IT'S GOT NOTHING TO DO WITH FUCKING COLOURED PEOPLE. I DON'T WANT TO BE AN ACADEMIC. THEY'RE NOT COLOURED ANYWAY. STOP PRETENDING THAT EVERYTHING WILL BE FINE IF I JUST BECOME LIKE YOU?!

Conor hangs up in fury. It takes a minute of hyperventilation to calm down, but he feels no relief. After another thirty seconds, he collects himself and murmurs

- They're not bloody coloured, anyway. You can't say that anymore. They're people of colour. Fucking dinosaur. People of colour.

Unfortunately, Conor is not shouting by the time he offers this important clarification. His father doesn't hear him. Nor do any nearby staff at the School of English. Nor indeed do any students outside: students full of ideas about patriarchy and cultural oppression and verbal violence; students offended by Conor's ignorance of his privilege and keen to castigate him for it.

You see, Sam's not there. She left when she heard him use two racial slurs — not one, but TWO. And — fuck! — if she's right, one of them was n—!

And it doesn't matter that she's completely misheard, because…. N——. Jesus! You can't even print that anymore, you know.

Chapter Seven

Dr Gisela Guzmán compresses the squeeze cap, desperately trying to draw out the last dregs of the tube. It takes both hands, but she gets the tinted moisturiser out eventually. It sits gloopy and cool on the tip of her finger. Her trip to the make-up store is delayed for another day.

It's a reminder of harder times. Times when expensive tubes were cut open so that none of their expensive elixir was wasted. Times when buying make-up meant less food in the house. Times when she still hoped her deadbeat dad might turn up at college with a magic wand and a bag of dollars.

She mixes the dark liquid with plain, white moisturiser. Make it go further, she thinks. Just like the old times. Because she wouldn't wish those hard times away, she thinks. Not for a second. They made her what she is today.

The dark and the white mix and, suddenly, there's a beautiful colour shining on her hand. Pure gold, she thinks, shining in the light.

Now for her face. So blotchy — so uneven — so *pale*.

She rubs in the mixture: round and round, round and round; first the cheeks, then the forehead. She feels like a great painter when she does this: round and round, round and round; making sure the colour's all mixed right, making sure it doesn't look streaky. It's a lot of work, but it's worth it.

She takes her hands off her face. And there it is — transformed.

Not blotchy — not grey. A uniform and clean colour — a sheen, a lustre. She's got a cool leather jacket and a cute new necklace. But all of that would be nothing without her skin. Her beautiful skin.

Pure gold, she thinks. Pure gold.

***

Pure bollocks, thinks John Bonnar. What a load of bollocks.

In another part of South Dublin, the former star of *True Kent Detective* hands his umbrella to the doorman and enters the lobby. The restaurant is one of those places with tiny biscuits and two Michelin stars. It's known for its stylish strawberry desserts.

More well-dressed fruits than Brighton, Bonnar said to the cabbie on the way up. Haha! The cabbie didn't really laugh.

As he walks to his table, whispers trail his bald head like snakes. Upmarket folk turning heads, purring at his sight. 'Is that…' he hears. The host of *Woke Watch*? A great broadcaster? The parliamentary candidate for the City of Chester?

But no. It comes, inevitably, as night follows day: 'Falmouth Smart? Is that Falmouth Smart? You know, the detective. No, it's not on anymore. On daytime repeat, maybe.'

Pure bollocks, he thinks. What a load of bollocks.

Waiting at his table is Oisín Mooney, a grin as thick as cream dolloped on his face.

- John, he says.
- Oisín.
- How are you? Enjoying Dublin?
- Yes, lovely. Very dirty.
- Ah, it's great isn't it? Why would you wanna be anywhere else? What have you been doing?
- Well, perusing mostly. I enjoyed the whiskey tasting.
- Jameson's, was it?
- Yeah.
- You made the right decision there. Stay away from Bushmills, Oisín winks…

Bonnar smiles politely.

-   …Course Jameson was a dirty Prod like yourself, but don't tell the American tourists. Did you walk up here? Smell the malt from the Guinness factory?

-   No. Cab.

-   Shame. Best thing in Dublin.

Bonnar says nothing. Oisín cops on.

-   Anyway, business, says Oisín. You're a busy man.

-   Right, says Bonnar.

-   I've got something interesting for you…

Oisín leans back in his chair and grins.

-   …It's about Dr Guzmán.

***

The door swings slowly behind her, weighted heavily so that it closes on its own. Dr Guzmán hears the door creak as she scans through her handbag. Looks for what she needs. Foundation. There. Hot sauce. There. But wait: where's her—

She cuts off her thought. Flicks frantically through her things. Tosses the make-up wipes aside. Throws out the mini mirror.

But it's not there.

She spins around like a ballet dancer, jumps, and wedges her foot into the gap between the door and the wall. Feels a jolt of pain as the old, heavy door crunches into her high-heeled foot.

As she gets back into the hallway, though, she congratulates herself. A bit drastic maybe, but she couldn't forget her phone.

Maybe it would be better if it wasn't like that — fewer toxic spats, fewer hate messages, fewer headaches from scrolling in the back of taxis.

But you need to be on social media. That's just what an academic does. That's just the way it is.

***

At another table, an elderly couple are grinning. They've just got Falmouth Smart — well, the actor who played him — to sign a napkin. He wasn't too happy about it, but he still did it.

At *this* table, however, Bonnar has tuned it all out. His red face displays a distinguished, puffy snarl.

- This is extremely important, he says, looking into Oisín's eyes. In a way, we are fighting for the soul of the West.

- Right, good, says Oisín. And that's why I've got you here short notice, you know. So the rub of it is—

He is interrupted by a white-jacketed waiter, approaching the table with two plates of tiny biscuits. The tiny biscuits are placed on the table.

- Your starters, gentlemen, says the waiter.

- Thanks, says Oisín.

Bonnar ignores the tiny biscuits: his thoughts seem to be collecting. There's a good chance he's gearing up for another Falmouth-Smart-style monologue.

Oisín flashes a quick look at the auld watch. Then back up to Bonnar, who's in his own world. Thank God, thinks Oisín. Got away with it.

- What we are doing is not just protesting an individual case, says Bonnar. We are unweaving the whole spool of logic which these people, over the course of decades, have spun.

- You're not wrong there John. So what I wanted to say was—

- What we now call woke has antecedents going back for over sixty years — perhaps longer, beyond Foucault even. By taking on Guzmán, we're not just highlighting one idiotic academic, we're exposing the whole twisted logic of this worldview. We are showing that this toxic ideology is cruel, silly, and at the bottom of it… why are you looking at your watch?

- Oh, nothing, sorry. Just a new watch.

A pause.

   - What did you bring me here for? Bonnar asks.

   - Right. So have a look at Twitter. Search 'Conor Crowley.'

   - Why? says Bonnar breathily.

   - You won't regret it, John. Just do it.

   - Okay.

He looks at the phone like a vicar examining a topless calendar.

   - Conor Crowley, he says slowly, typing with one finger.

He peruses for a second, then his eyes flash up.

   - My god, Bonnar says. At the university? 'Verbal violence.' Is that one of Conor's students trying to get him cancelled? Christ alive.

   - Even better, John. I know him. And I know for a fact he's not the type to say anything out of order. He doesn't care about any of this woke stuff, either way…

Oisín leans in.

   - …And guess who his supervisor is?

Bonnar is grinning.

   - Wait… This is Dr Guzmán's student? The one who's your friend?

   - Yes indeed. And even better than that. Guess who's giving a presentation tomorrow?

   - No?

   - And she'll be there too.

Bonnar leans back in his chair. A wide, satisfied grin — the kind you might see on a ruddy boy at a prep-school Prizegiving — fills up his face. Then it fills the room. Oisín grins back at him, laughing.

   - Well, says Bonnar, it looks like we'll have to change our plan…

   - Case closed! says Oisín, rather too excitedly.

Bonnar's smile evaporates.

***

- Gisela, it's fantastic to see you.

Professor Darcy, Head of the School of English, gets up from his seat and holds out his hand. He wears a crisp white shirt buttoned up stiffly and tight trousers and on his pinkish face are rectangular glasses which highlight smart, cynical eyes. He's tall and wiry but his hands look bulky — the legacy of endless teenage hours on the rugby field.

They're in the Staff Common Room, a big scarlet lounge filled with leather chairs and polished wood tables. On the ceiling hangs an ancient Venetian chandelier: a legacy of the days when there was money to be had at the university.

The room smells like the Victorian age — arsenic and all. It's late, and they're the only two in there. There's a little box on one of the tables where staff can request any wine in the world. Of course, no one does that anymore. There's also a grand piano in the corner. But no one plays it.

Dr Guzmán offers him a tentative hand. She notices the softness of his grip and, feeling calmer, folds into it.

- How are you? she asks.
- Oh, you know, says Professor Darcy. The kids are a full-time job. Hate leaving Saoirse to it…

He pulls his hand away, unaffected.

- …Anyway, he continues, just to say…

His voice is flat with a hint of ruthlessness.

- …congratulations. You're our newest Associate Professor.

Dr Guzmán's eyelids leap and her arms stretch for the sky.

- Fantastic! She says. Thank you, Patrick! Thank you!

She jumps at him for an impromptu hug. He winces as her arms wrap around him.

- I can't tell you how much this means to me, she says.
- That's okay, he says. Very well earnt. Very long overdue…

She laughs and smiles.

- …We should've had more diversity in the department a long time ago.

In a split second her eyes darken and she frowns at the floor. She holds her eyes there for a moment, but within seconds she's up again and flashing a smile at him. This time, it's fake.

- Yeah, she says, of course.

Whatever. A job's a job — and this is a *great* job. This is what she's always wanted.

- So congratulations, he says. This little number is yours. He hands her a brass name plate.

Dr Gisela Guzmán

Associate Professor in English Literature

- Thank you, she says.

- You've a pay rise with this, plus the opportunity to employ one of your research students. It's pretty good money, he says.

- Oh damn, she says. That reminds me. Conor. He's been accused of—

- Wait, says Darcy. How do you already know about—

- It's already on Twitter. The student posted it. Samantha Kunz-O'Connell.

- She did? Jesus. That quickly. I… I…

He takes his glasses off and puts them back on again.

- …I didn't think that would get out. At least not this quickly. Jesus. Jesus… what do you think?

- I don't know. You're the Head of English.

- I know. But you're the…

He pauses, unsure whether he can say it, then goes ahead. Why shouldn't he?

- …woman of colour.

- So?

- So…

- I can't make those decisions for you, Professor Darcy, she says.

- Right, he says. Right. Any advice though?

- I'm not your Racism Advisor, Professor Darcy. I'm your Associate Professor. You hired me to teach English.
- Right, okay, okay. You're right, he says.

His eyes dart around.

- Well, I'll take the decision. We don't have the precedent to suspend someone for this. It... it...

He looks to her for support or dissent. She keeps her face dead straight. Not your Racism Advisor, she thinks.

- ...I'll make the decision, he says. We don't... we don't have the precedent to suspend. The presentation goes ahead.

He looks at her for approval. Right decision? his eyes seem to ask.

Wrong decision, she thinks. But she doesn't say it. Let him make his own mistakes. She's an Associate Professor now. She won't do his dirty work for him.

She smiles. But she also won't be afraid to call him out, she thinks. *When the time's right.*

- Anyway, he says, I better get back to the kids. The presentation goes ahead. We inform the student. We kick it down the road until next Friday.
- Okay, says Dr Guzmán, giving away nothing.
- Goodbye, he says, and turns to leave.

He walks towards the piano, besides which a huge nineteenth-century doorway stands.

- Oh, he says. And congratulations, Gisela.

Professor Darcy smiles weakly then walks into the dark corridor. For a minute Dr Guzmán is stood alone in the room, the chandelier shining brightly above her.

***

Two hours later, Conor's at home having a bath. He's re-drafting apologies to Katie on his phone, trying to forget about the missed calls from his dad, trying to forget about the presentation, trying to forget about everything.

Then he gives up. There's just no way he's gonna convince Katie. The fact of the matter is he's a prick.

He checks Twitter. Sees some scandal about an academic somewhere. Poor bastard.

Then he checks Gmail and sees a message from the Head of English. He drops his phone in the bath.

Allegations of verbal violence. Possible suspension. Decision made next week. Oof.

Chapter Eight

It's the morning of the presentation. Conor lies in bed, sleeping uneasily, shaking like a spider in the bedsheets.

In his dream, a cavalcade progresses. A horde of open-top cars drive by, each marked in huge letters 'NO OMISSIONS (RACIALLY SPEAKING).' He looks on from the pavement, stuck in a sea of spectators. Each person claps with glee, trying to outdo everyone else, but each one is out of focus and Conor cannot see anything but a crowd.

The cavalcade rumbles through the streets without end. Conor notices a float full of kids in *Nike* activewear. It's his students, led by Samantha Kunz-O'Connell. She stands at the back of the float dressed like a Miss World contestant and holds a placard out to the crowd which says simply 'POSITIONALITY.' The rest of his students are on their phones.

Next, he sees a gigantic Popemobile enlarged to accommodate fifteen people. Inside are besuited businessmen sipping strawberry daquiris.

Conor can't make out any of them until he sees a grin much like that of a cult leader about to order a mass suicide. Oisín Mooney, waving to the crowd. Oisín's every move is covered by a camera crew, beaming his performance onto every social network.

Crew Slut by Frank Zappa rings out, except with politically correct lyrics. Oisín, wearing a grey suit and a gold dollar-sign chain, starts to dance.

***

Suddenly, Conor is sitting in a massive athletics stadium. He looks down to the running track where some athletes are limbering up. One of the athletes is Dr Guzmán. Like the rest of them, she's wearing *Nike* activewear.

In the centre, there is a podium on which the businessmen stand discussing matters amongst themselves. They are headed once again by Oisín Mooney, who runs around the podium highfiving the crowd.

On the right, though, is a news desk at which a red-faced male sits furiously. He wears the uniform of the Kent Police Force, and his desk is inscribed with the name 'Falmouth Smart'.

Oisín pulls a few dance moves for the cheering crowd until a henchman hands him a cowboy hat and a script. He puts it on and starts reading.

Oisín: YEEE-HAW! Most of you already know me but for those who don't, I'll say a few words.

D—! F—! P—y!

(LAUGHTER FROM CROWD).

Oisín: I would like to take this opportunity to acknowledge that this hot shindig takes place on the ancestral and unceded territory of some f—— tribe!

(MOMENT OF SILENT REFLECTION)

Yeeeeeeeeeeeeeeeeeeeeeeeeeeeeeeeeeeeeeeeeeeeeeeeeee ee-haw! I'm the Head Sponsor and Supreme Leader, Oisín Mooney. But isn't that obvious?

(TIPS HIS COWBOY HAT AND THRUSTS HIS HIPS TO THE CROWD

Yeeeeeeeeeeeeeeeeeeeeeeeeee-haw! I don't like this woke bullshit, but I'm gonna pretend to like it. Why? Because the kids who buy my bulls— picked it up on Instagram! Does that sound good?

(CHEERS)

That's why I'm so proud to lead our coalition of sponsors: *Corporations for Oriental Slave Labour and also Social*

Justice. We bring you Social Justice because we care about money! Uighurs: get in the re-education camps!

Oisín dances to Wet Ass Pussy by Cardi B, except with politically correct lyrics.

Crowd (as one): WHO ARE THE UIGHURS?!

Oisín (dancing whitely): Pussy-ass b—s with no f——— disposable income!

Oisín grabs his earpiece, then nods gravely.

What's your take on this, Falmouth Smart?

The camera cuts to the red-faced man at the news desk. The man wears a suit and tie with aggressively traditional hair. He looks into the camera and tuts with fury.

Falmouth Smart: Well this is utter garbage. I've been dragged to see this — dragged to see this by my producers. This is ridiculous. Absolutely absurd. I don't want to watch it. It's morally and intellectually defunct. Terrible. Ridiculous.

Oisín: Thanks for that hot take, Falmouth.

Oisín dances to *Amhrán na bhFiann*, except with politically correct lyrics. Now, without further ado, let's get the ball f— moving! Athletes, take your motherf— marks!

The athletes take their marks and show off their doctorates. Conor recognises Dr Guzmán.

Ready, set, go!

Oisín fires the starting pistol, killing several. The athletes roll around in agony… but the shots were fired into the crowd, not the race.

Athlete 1: The race is rigged!

Athlete 2: The race is rigged against ME!

Dr Guzmán: I used to hate people of colour, but then I was diversity trained! Now I hate myself!

(CHEERS)

Men are not better at math!

(CHEERS)

Sexuality is a spectrum!

(CHEERS)

We are all the same!

(STANDING OVATIONS)

Actually… we're not all the same!

Dr Guzmán is crowned by Oisín. Both pose for photographs with the Nike © WET_POWER 2022 collection. The other athletes are executed by the Chinese government.

Oisín: A quick announcement. Buy © Pepsi and end racial injustice!

(DRINKS CAN OF © PEPSI-COLA. SPITS IT OUT. VOMITS. RESUMES DANCING.)

Now, over to you Falmouth Smart.

Falmouth Smart (scoffingly): I mean what on earth are they thinking? If you didn't think the woke mob had gone too far, now, my friends: you know! I mean *'come on!'* This is the biggest intellectual *turd* yet dropped by humanity. Now what if I told you that © Pepsi-Cola is the most refreshing drink in the world? What would you think?! Well, my friends: it is! I've been drinking it for yonks now — can't get through a show without it! Love it! Now back to Oisín.

Oisín: Thanks Falmouth. *Corporations for Oriental Slave Labour and also Social Justice* are proud to present you with the Social Justice Gold Medal! You Lose! You also win the Man Booker Prize, an interview in *Teen Vogue,* and a place at our new Business School! Congratulations! Look how shiny this f——— medal is! It's like colonialism never happened!

(Dr Guzmán is crowned)

Dr Guzmán: The race was rigged against me and I still lost!

Conor: How can the race be rigged against you? You're a Doctor of the Arts. You teach at a university. (To everyone) You *all* teach at universities! You're *all* Professors!

Crowd (booing): It's a competition!

Conor: What's the point of competing to see who is most oppressed?

Crowd (in righteous fury): They're more oppressed than you?

Conor: But I'm not oppressed at all! I'm just weak!

Falmouth Smart: I mean, come on! I tell you what though, if that mob gets quiet, I tell you what — I'll be out of a job! Case closed!

The stadium erupts. Case closed! They yelp. Case closed!

Among the throng of noise, Conor notices that he has no teeth and is naked. Then he sees his dad standing next to him.

Peter Crowley: They've got a point, you know. Now how's the presentation going?

***

- AAAAAAAAAAAAAAAAAAAAAAAAAAAAAAAAAA AAAAAAAAAAAAAAH!

Our handsome hero has just woken up. It's the morning of the presentation, which begins at 10AM. He looks at his phone: 9:30. In his troubled dreams, he's overslept. He looks out the window and hears light rain falling on the street outside.

Half a cup of tea later and he's out the door, stumbling his way to campus while also tying his shoes and zipping up his coat. The early morning seagulls squawk at the uncollected rubbish.

There's a buzz in one of his pockets, but he's got so fucking many of them that he can't find his phone. After an ecstasy of fumbling, he gets it, but fuck! it's Oisín calling. He won't be hearing about the bad dream, thinks Conor, nor the fact that he might be suspended from the university.

He picks up the phone.

- Hello Conor, says Oisín. I'm just calling to let you know how fucked it is that they might suspend you. And I've got a surprise for you, too—
- What?
- Well I think this campaign to cancel you is—
- How do you know about that?
- It was all over Twitter. Didn't you see?
- But they didn't name me?

- Of course they did. The students did. Everyone knows it's you.

- Hold on a second, Conor says, almost stumbling into a pissed-off seagull…

He checks the School of English Twitter page.

- …but they didn't put me on their page?

- Look at the thread, says Oisín.

- Christ! How can they get away with naming me like that?

- That's awful! I'll make a note. It'll be brilliant for our case.

The line cuts out a little as Conor turns onto Dominick Street. Grey sky hangs over him as a seagull chomps through a green bin bag.

- What? Our case? Conor replies.

- Against censorship, bro.

- What censorship?

- I haven't told you yet, but—

- Told me what?

- You should be able to put whatever you want in your doctorate, regardless of political correctness.

- But Oisín, my doctorate hasn't got anything to do with political correctness. I just said—

- Exactly, and you weren't allowed to express an opinion, were you?

- It's not about my doctorate! I just said 'coloured' instead of 'people of colour' because I was angry.

- Exactly! Although…

Oisín pauses like a PR man.

- …between you and me Conor, you should really stop saying 'coloured'. Even if you are angry. I'd deny it if I were you.

- I didn't use it. I was correcting my da—

- Right, exactly. I mean you don't have to deny it with me, just in public.

- I was correcting him!

- Of course. Anyway, listen Conor. You have to meet me in Campus Square before the presentation. I've got a surprise for you. This is gonna be huge. It's gonna be all over Twitter.

- I don't want it to be all over Twitter, I just want a job.

- Exactly! So meet me at the square in fifteen minutes.

- I've got to—

Oisín hangs up.

Bastard! Thinks Conor. The bastard! Oisín showed zero interest in his career, zero interest in his problems, zero interest in his person. But now he's sniffed some kind of legal opportunity. He wants to turn himself into Johnnie Cochran — and Conor has to be fucking OJ.

He turns off Moore Street as shouts of 'cigarettes' and 'tobacco' bounce off the low buildings. Then after a moment he's at O'Connell Street with the great ugly Spire stealing his view. He pulls up the hood of his coat against the drizzle. He's heading, against his better instincts, for the university.

As he rushes by the GPO he sees a tricolour hanging proudly over a sleeping homeless man. He steps out into the road then steps back quickly as the grey-orange flash of the LUAS fills his vision. Ten minutes later and he's stepping into the university entrance and walking past a gaggle of tourists.

The campus view presents itself. A grand chapel in which nobody worships. An eighteenth century building that's now luxury accommodation. A statue of a proud man who used his intellectual might to support slavery. It's all wearing a bit thin at this grand old university.

Behind Campus Square, the spire of the new Business School looms buzzard-like. Suddenly Oisín's voice hits Conor like a kick in the bollocks.

- Over here, Conor! Over here!

He looks across the square where Oisín stands. Conor wants to walk on by, but he figures he should ask what's up — after all, it's gonna involve him whether he likes it or not.

- What is it? Conor asks.

He checks his watch: 9:50. The presentation is in ten minutes, but it should only take two or three to get to the room where he's due to present. He'll still have time to skim through his notes, which is good because he can't remember the title.

Oisín raises his arms to the heavens. Behind him are the ancient buildings of the university and the wide, cobbled square. The fine rain grows thicker.

- Welcome to the circus, bro, he says. This is how I bail you out.

- Oisín, seriously, I don't want to be part of this, I just want to get out without everyone hating me.

- Isn't that what you've been doing your whole life, bro? asks Oisín. Trying not to offend people?

He lets his arms fall slowly to his sides.

- I don't know, Oisín. I've got a presentation, Conor says.

- And then what?

- I don't know, okay?

- Exactly, so let me tell you about the movement we're starting.

- And what business exactly do you have starting a movement?

- *Toiraidh na hÉireann.* It's from the Irish word for 'outlaw,' because we're outlawed by the political mainstream.

- Answer the question, Oisín. Why are you starting a movement?

- They're starting a TV station in the UK. Anti-woke. They're gonna give us a spot.

- So what? Who cares?

- There's good money in it, says Oisín.

Conor looks at his wide-eyed friend.

- And what do you want me for?

- You don't wanna do this woke university bullshit, do you Conor? Why don't you join us? We might not be an institution, but at least we're not so unsure of ourselves that we'll accept any guilt-tripping ideology that gets thrown our way.

    - But why this anti-woke stuff?

    - It'll be in demand in the next few years.

    - Do you actually believe all that, Oisín?

    - More than all that PC bollocks.

    - Come on, man. Downfall of the West. Clash of civilisations. Surely you don't take that seriously?

Oisín looks at Conor's manuscript, dampening in the drizzle.

    - Do I take it seriously? What about you? You work at a college. You work for people who believe they're in some holy war against a racist, patriarchal, whateverist tyranny. Do I take it seriously? I could ask you the same question.

Conor screws up his face and grips the manuscript tightly enough to scrunch it. He's about to turn and walk away when, like a sunrise after a coke binge, Sam Kunz-O'Connell rampages into view.

    - You asshole! She shouts. You asshole! She repeats, somewhat unnecessarily.

Conor is shocked that she's making the point with so much force. He's never seen political correctness expressed in such a visceral manner, but then he hasn't read *The Guardian* in a while.

    - Come on, Sam, he says as she cannonballs towards him… but he's interrupted by her swinging fist.

Imagine his surprise when it smashes into Oisín instead of him. The first bit of luck he's had all year.

    - You asshole! She shouts, again unnecessarily.

    - Sam, what are you doing? This is my friend, says Conor.

    - Why am I not surprised you know this asshole?!

Conor mouth drops in confusion.

    - How do you know him? he asks.

    - You know already, don't you? Asshole! You're trying to insult me even more.

- I really don't.
- My sister. Laura O'Connell. You probably even knew her when she went here. Asshole.
- Her last name's different, Oisín says, who is now attempting to cower behind Conor.
- Wait, says Conor, the girl you pissed yourself in front of? The one you slept w... she was Sam's sis—

But Sam interrupts before Oisín can do anything more than nod.

- I already told you why I changed my name to Kunz-O'Connell. I added my mom's last name to challenge the patriarchy.
- The patriarchy must be really reeling from that blow, says Oisín.

This is followed by a groan as Sam's elbow meets Oisín's stomach.

- Asshole!

Conor attempts to come between them.

- For God's sake, Sam. I know he's an arsehole, but...

Conor tries to think of a good reason why she should stop hitting him. He tries, and tries, and tries, but it's too hard — and soon enough his thoughts are arrested as her furious foot crashes into Oisín's groin.

- ...attacking him isn't going to help! Jesus!
- Taking his side, huh? You're a racist!
- It doesn't matter if I'm racist, you're beating the shit out of him!

A crowd of bemused phones has helpfully appeared in the square to film the whole scene. Sam stops beating him for a second and looks at Conor.

- And you're an asshole too! You knew all along, didn't you?
- No! says Conor.

That's enough, he thinks. He has to get to the presentation.

Our handsome hero heroically runs away as Sam shouts behind him

- You're a racist asshole! That's why I put it on Twitter… and now you're gonna lose your job! I bet you'll lose your girlfriend too.

Conor runs on but shouts over his shoulder

- You don't know what you're talking about! I can't get a girlfriend! And I don't have a job!

Just as he's getting out of earshot, he hears Oisín's limp voice calling after him.

- Wait for the surprise, Conor!

After that, Conor's sure that he hears something about detective dramas and critical race theory and the downfall of the West… followed by a whimper.

***

Every now and then a man faces the fact that, in the grand rhythms of the universe, he is utterly pointless.

This is now the unfortunate fate of Conor as he steps into the lecture hall, ready to instruct the crowd awaiting his presentation with hushed lips. No one has even noticed his arrival, though: they're all nibbling horrid little pastries.

He can't even find Dr Guzmán. She hasn't got here on time.

The Head of English, Professor Darcy, is in the midst of a speech. He makes a joke which garners some exhalations then walks off stage shaking his head. Clearly it will be a splendid morning.

Still, the room is packed by the standards of the School of English: half-full, or half-empty if you take the more realistic view. Most of the faces Conor doesn't recognise: probably the friends and family of the students due to talk after him. All of them are happily chatting except for one solitary figure, sat alone at the back.

The man wears a wax jacket below two grave eyebrows and a shiny red head. In his right hand there is a cherry wood umbrella. Conor cannot see his face, though, because the man's view is directed firmly at the ground.

As Conor's wondering when he'll be called up, Dr Guzmán's thump fills his ears. She takes a coffee from a waitress without saying thank you then walks straight past him, over to Professor Darcy. She apologizes for being late.

- But then again, time is a white concept, she chortles.

Darcy returns the chortle — uneasily. But his amusement is curtailed by a weedy English medievalist clearing his throat into the onstage microphone. Conor remembers that he once saw this guy literally picking his nose in the School of English Common Room.

- So, without further ado — is it ado or adue? I never know, heh heh…

The crowd rejects his joke unequivocally.

- … let's welcome our first doctoral candidate. Conor Crowley!

A few solitary claps echo as Conor comes to the podium. He gulps. Wonders whether they know. Then he realises that his notes are soaking wet, with the ink bleeding all over the page. None of the words are legible.

He'll just have to do without, he thinks, clearing his throat. The fact is that, although he doesn't want to be an academic, he does want to have a job, he does want to have a salary, and he does want to pay for his own burritos. So, notes or no notes, he's doing the presentation.

- Hello, he says.

Then he hits a stumbling block. He's not exactly sure what the presentation says. He knows the key arguments, but he can't just translate them into spoken English at the drop of a hat. In fact, what was the title?

- Araby: Orientalism, Appropriation, and… Resistance… in Irish Literature of the 1910s, he says. In James Joyce, he adds. Dubliners.

It was something like that anyway. Maybe he added that little 'Resistance' because it sounds like something Dr Guzmán would say.

With the title out of the way, Conor expects that everything else will fall into place. He waits patiently for a minute for this to happen — but it doesn't. Meanwhile, an unvanquishable urge rushes up from his bladder to his brain and back down again. It takes tangible shape and presses on him like a trapped animal as he jerks around in a piss dance for five seconds or more.

   - Uh, he says.

Excellent start: now the rest of the hour. He clears his throat once more: if he can just get in as many buzzwords as possible...

He speaks.

   - If, for a while, academic study of the Irish Literary Revival, and the Irish Revolutionary Period in general is heuristic, soon the narrative of marginal, exoticising binaries... you know, requires a colonial way of... of looking at the whole thing. As Edward Said said. Shit, I mean Edward 'Sayeeeed'. As Edward Sayeeeed said. Um.

For reasons unknown to Conor a cerebral section of the front row perks up. He's not sure if they're big Edward Said fans or if they somehow understood him.

He pauses for a moment as an image flashes up in his brain. A great crowd. Multitudes of people — multitudes upon multitudes — who care nothing about Araby, Orientalism, or anything else he's mentioned. Dublin cab drivers. Fun-fair managers. Arabs.

How do they get on with it? Clothe themselves, feed themselves, stagger to reproduce. How is that? He can see them in his mind now, looking at him with quizzical eyes, asking why he didn't study Business.

It's not so much that this stuff has nothing to say to normal people — it's that it's not even trying. Maybe all these words do have meaning, but is there not a way to say the same

thing without creating a ridiculous new language? And if
these academics are for the people, why are they so difficult to
understand?

It suddenly strikes Conor that he doesn't want to be here.
So if he can just hold the room for a while, he might be able
to slip off for a piss. Then he realises that he doesn't need to
piss anymore.

   - Uh, says Conor again.

He looks out the window. The rain has stopped and,
through the dark cloud, snatches of blue are visible. If he
could only get outside…

Then an American whine pierces the air: the voice of Dr
Guzmán.

   - I'm sorry, folks, but I can't let you go on with this. As
a member of the Afro-Latinx community…

That hard 'x' throws off the older members of the
audience somewhat. As bemused looks fly around the room,
though, she comes up on stage and takes the lectern off
Conor.

   - … I cannot stand by while this goes on. This should
not be going ahead. The fact that the School of English has
not made a notice of suspension for this student is creating
real harm and making this campus unsafe for people of—

   - FRAUD!

A male voice. Gasps from the crowd. Dr Guzmán
inhaling audibly.

Conor sneaks a look at his watch: 10:35. The
supermarkets will be selling lager by now. If he can just get
off stage, into the aisle and out the door…

   - Afro-Latinx?

The voice is upper-class, English, and tingles with polite
anger. Its owner now reveals himself. He's bald-headed with a
crimson face and a pinstripe suit out of which a handkerchief
dangles pointlessly. He stands at the back and, as the crowd's
attention diverts to him, walks purposefully into the aisle. The

man from before, thinks Conor: the one who sat alone in his wax jacket. But where's the jacket now?

- Afro-Latinx… And what exactly does this rather flowery language signify?

She stares into space, gobsmacked.

- I'm sure that the audience would appreciate a little explanation. After all, he says slowly, we are not all quite so up to date on the hottest academic trends as yourself.

She looks wide-eyed into the crowd as mutters rise from it like steam from a kettle. The man, meanwhile, paces up the aisle, scuppering Conor's plan to get out. The man opens his mouth again.

- You see, ladies and gentlemen, this language can often be rather overwhelming for small people such as ourselves. But— unless I am mistaken —Afro-Latinx is a term used to describe a person of mixed Hispanic and African origin. We have discarded the term 'Latino' because, following Spanish convention, the masculine includes the feminine. Allowing a language to exist outside English gender conventions is just too painful for… somebody. Would that be correct, Dr Guzmán?

He doesn't give her time to answer.

- But I query Dr Guzmán's use of this term Afro-Latino — I'm sorry: 'Latinx' — for one simple reason. I have reason to believe that she is not all she says she is.

- Stop! shouts Dr Guzmán from the lectern. Stop this imposter!

The man walks slowly and inexorably up the aisle, towards the lectern at which Dr Guzmán now freezes in anguish. He slows his walk for drama and at intervals strokes his chin with a sombre right hand.

- But is it I who imposts, Dr Guzmán? Or is it thee? Because I have reason to believe that you are not, in fact, an Afro-Latina woman. I have reason to believe that you are, in fact… pretending!

He snaps a privately-educated finger at her as the crowd gasps in unison.

- Are you not a Jewish woman from Fort Collins, Colorado?! Is your name not Judith Griesmann? Is this whole façade not just another lie that you have told in order to exploit the guilty liberals who run our universities?! Did you not invent this whole Afro-Latina identity in order to further your career as a left-wing academic?!

With impeccable timing, he now turns to the crowd.

- My name is John Bonnar and I am here on behalf of the Union of Free Speech Activists. You see, there is a lie being told here. Judith Griesmann was born to a German father and a white American mother — and this... is Judith Griesmann...

He points at her.

- ...She is as white as — it seems — everyone in this room.

An Indian chap in the centre smiles awkwardly as the crowd prolongs its gasp.

- She has been pretending to be a black Latina woman for ten years now, aided by brown make up and a guilty liberal establishment. Academia has lapped it up, lauding her for her — and I quote — 'effortless application of Critical Race Theory to the cultural politics of medieval jousting.'

***

As phones pop out to film the kerfuffle, Professor Darcy, the Head of English, stares from his seat with great anxiety. He cannot, however, summon the authority to step in and shut the whole thing down.

- At the Union of Free Speech Activists, we work to protect those who have been abandoned by the mainstream media...

As Conor watches the speech, he thinks about whether he's seen this guy before. There's something faintly recognisable about him, like the smell of piss on the corner of a street. But where has he seen him?

2006, was it? Around then? — Definitely around the time of Tony Blair's swansong. He searches his mind. A detective drama he watched with his mum and dad, was it? The one that aired on Sunday nights before *Top Gear*. He and his dad loved the mystery but his mum was always complaining about the show's 'implied Tory politics.' Was it him?

Conor watches from the stage. Bonnar is in full flow now with his shiny crimson head bobbing up and down as he goes for the rhetorical jugular. It was him! Conor thinks. He played the lead in that detective show!

Conor remembers seeing this kind of lecture every episode — usually at the end, as Bonnar's character unmasked another Kentish nonce.

That was it! Falmouth Smart was the name of the detective. He'd been the top detective in the Met, but he was transferred out to Kent after stretching the rules on a hard case one time too many. *True Kent Detective* — what a show.

- Here at the Union of Free Speech Activists, we believe that wokery is ruining our country. When you accept moral lessons from someone on the basis of their identity, do you not leave yourself vulnerable to any old nonsense dressed up in fancy language? Indeed, do you not leave yourself vulnerable to any old scamster dressed up in curly hair and dark makeup..?

...And where does that leave free speech? Where is free speech in the university here, or at universities in any other part of our country?

A few in the crowd look mildly pissed off. Is he suggesting that Ireland and the UK are the same country? On the other hand, it seems that most of them are willing to give him a pass given the drama of events.

- I think that most ordinary people would agree with me that this is absurd, although perhaps not here in the ivory academic towers of...

He flicks through his notes as he searches for the name. Finally he comes up with

- …this once great institution!

It's at this stage that Conor notices the small camera crew at the back of the lecture hall. Plus all the phones hoisted at Dr Guzmán — or whatever her real name is — as she stands there with defeat written in her eyes. Up here on the stage, Conor thinks, he'll be in the background of all their shots. Time to get out.

He walks crab-like towards the stage's exit. At the same time, Bonnar's speech really gets serious. He talks about grade inflation, pastoral care, the enemies of Western civilisation. Then he brings up Winston Churchill. Typical Brit, Conor hears whispered in the crowd, the only dates they know are 1940 and 1966.

He closes in on the edge of the stage. If he can just get down the aisle to the door while the cameras are on Bonnar…

- And how dare you come to the presentation of your own student to denounce him to the thought police!

Everyone looks at Conor, who freezes just as he's about to hop off stage. So close.

- I have it on good authority that Ms Griesmann has been forcing her ideology on this student. Is this not censorship in the universities?

What good authority? Conor asks himself. Then he picks out a figure from the crowd at the back of the room, bubbling with excitement as he holds Bonnar's umbrella and wax jacket. The figure grins and gives Conor a big thumbs up, his face ever so slightly purple. Of course, thinks Conor. Oisín — Oisín and his 'movement.'

- What do you say to that, Conor? asks Bonnar.

The eyes in the room pincer in. Silence extends. Conor notices he's not saying anything.

- Uh… he finally offers. It isn't considered satisfactory.

The crowd waits.

- Well, um, Sir Falmouth—

- Falmouth?
- Sorry!
- Well?
- Well…
- What do you think about this censorship?

Oisín beams at Conor from the back row, happy and doglike. He seems to be mouthing something for Conor to say, but Conor can't make it out and, even if he could, it wouldn't matter.

He doesn't want to be an academic. The atmosphere around him would be so toxic that he'd spend years depoliticising himself. An image flashes into his brain of himself aged eighty, legs weak from lack of use, bitching about the latest development in theoretical studies.

Then he imagines all the squabbles he'd endure, the intellectual egoism, the 'I'm interesting' smugness that leaks like drool out of these peoples' mouths. He'll just say something now, leave, and never come back. Find the pub in Crumlin where his grandad used to drink, maybe.

- To be honest, I'm tired of all of you, Conor says. I don't think you're bad people. I don't even think you're stupid people. But I do think — and I don't know how to say this without sounding rude — I do think that you're not very important.

Bonnar guffaws some public-school-sounding encouragement. It must be some dialectical version of 'hear-hear.' Conor scowls back at him, but he doesn't even notice.

Then Conor looks out to the crowd. There's a few miserable females at the front, white with emotion, self-loathing painted in their eyes. Then there's the small group of smug-looking lads who seem to be supporting Bonnar, sat near the back like sulking schoolboys.

All of them say nothing.

There's the Indian chap in the centre, aware that his being the only non-white person has suddenly become important; aware also that Professor Darcy will make sure he's in every photo the School of English posts after this. And most evident of all, the people holding cameras, formless faces hidden behind their devices like they would choke without them. They all fade into one, some bearing weird hats or different t-shirts or dyed hair as if that might prove they're individuals; but all, nonetheless, a crowd.

Still they say nothing.

Conor feels like asking what they want from him. Why do they sit around all day searching for the most outrageous thing so that all their outraged friends can be outraged too? Do they like living in a virtual world of good and evil while, in the real world, their fertility plummets and the animals die because of their noxious fumes? What are their lives lacking that makes them so angry? What do they want from him? How do they want him to contribute to their dystopia?

He considers saying all these things as the silence reaches a crescendo. He pauses, looking for a glint of humanity in the crowd's eyes. But it's not there. Conor draws in a deep breath then says with perfect clarity as they look at him like some ancient prophet

-   I'm going to the pub.

Chapter Nine

From his office window, Professor Darcy throws a pensive gaze across Campus Square. The target of his stare is the new Business School, which stands tall and proud like a huge middle finger flipped at the less prosperous parts of the university.

It's dreadful to spend your life in the relentless pursuit of mediocrity. After twenty years in the game, Darcy commands the biggest office in a School of English which has had its budget cut three of the last five years. He works in a dingy brutalist building with bad wi-fi and rumours of asbestos that make him feel a lot like a big fish in a small pond. Upon elevation to Head of School, Darcy quickly discovered that a great deal of his job was making good people redundant while the Business School shot up magically next door.

He looks at the academic robes that hang next to his bookcase, then across his coffee-stained desk. Looking back at him is Conor Crowley, who has been called in following the debacle a few days ago. Our handsome hero isn't sure whether he's going to get suspended, cleared, or expelled — but he no longer cares. It's a year to the day since his mum died and he wants to get this over with. Call his dad.

Darcy displays all the symptoms of a long career in academia: the cynicism, the loss of ambition, the unshakeable look of a teenager who's never got old. But, in all his years working, he's never seen anything like this. An academic pretending to be black. An exposé on campus. An internet sensation that shows her caught out live on camera. He looks at Conor and sighs.

- Guzmán, he says. A Spanish surname of toponymic origin, derived from the village of Guzmán in northern Spain. Scholars once thought the name of Germanic origin, which is ironic in our case.

- Because of Dr Guzmán?

- Dr Griesmann. Her father, it turns out, was a German car salesman. Her mother was Jewish-American, from a small city in Colorado. That's where she grew up, learning Hebrew and celebrating a *bat mitzvah*. Sometime later she began to pass as Afro-Latina. But apparently she only has high school Spanish.

- I see, says Conor awkwardly.

Darcy slides a photo across his desk. It shows a group of teenagers at some celebration, a gawky girl smiling at the front with pale skin and limbs she's not sure what to do with. The other girls stand slightly away from her. In her flat smile Conor sees a hint of some unspoken sadness, difficult or impossible to articulate but nonetheless present and powerful.

- She never tried to censor me, Conor says. Just, like, convert me.

Darcy ignores the point.

- Can I ask you a question, Conor? In the spirit of free speech?

- I never had any problems w—

- Why do you think it's always Jewish people trying to be something else?

- I'm sorry?

- I mean, just to play devil's advocate, right?

- But what's the—

- Freedom of speech means the right to ask difficult questions, doesn't it? Here's the point. She stopped being Jewish; she started being black and Latino. Why? I don't know why. But she did. She un-Jewed herself.

A self-satisfied smile curls up his lips.

- So… you're asking me why she didn't want to be Jewish?

- Well, you're the kid who…

His fingers throw up air-quotes

- …'SLAMS down race faking SJW professor in front of crowd.' According to *Woke Watch* on YouTube.

- Yeah, I don't really… I think that was more Falmouth anyway. I wasn't—

- Falmouth?

- Shit — I mean, John Bonnar. I used to watch *True Kent Detective*. He played the…

Conor shakes his head…

- …It wasn't me. It was Bonnar.

- Well maybe we could do with someone to take on all this PC stuff around here.

- I don't quite see wh—

- The point is this, Conor. Why should we stop asking difficult questions on campus, even if they are unpleasant? I believe in free speech too. Look, at the end of this, I'm gonna offer you a job, so humour me. Isn't this exactly the type of question people are afraid to ask? Why is it that wherever you look, whether it's Trump or the Far Left, there's always people of that background pretending to be something else?

- I don't—

- Understand that I'm playing devil's advocate. These are questions that people shouldn't be afraid to ask — I mean, even if maybe they're questions that don't need to be asked.

- Okay.

Darcy ambles around his swivel chair.

- What I mean is you won't need to feel afraid in the new research role that—

- Thanks, but I'm not—

- You shouldn't be afraid to ask those questions. It's what academics are for.

Conor smiles awkwardly. Darcy leans in.

- You can ask this. You can ask whether debate's being shut down. You can ask these questions.

- I don't want to ask those—

- You have to understand: I'm playing devil's advocate. I'm using irony here. And— wait, what? You don't want to—

- Stop interrupting me, says Conor.

Silence hangs in the air with the smell of stale coffee.

- You don't want to work here? Darcy asks.

- No thanks.

- Oh.

The office suddenly feels stuffy and small. It's like the whole room has shrunk in on itself. Suddenly, Darcy's coffee-breath smells awfully close.

- Why? I mean, most doctoral students search everywhere for paid work after they finish. You're not even done yet. You'd be privileged to get this opportunity — if you excuse the 'woke' term.

His fingers flex sarcastic quote marks in the air. He's agitated: the yellow teeth prove it.

- No thanks, repeats Conor.

- What is it? Did another college offer you something first?

- I don't want to be an academic.

- Ha. Why not? Wanna get on YouTube? Try your luck on OnlyFans? Or is university a 'nightmare from which you are trying to awake'?

- I'd say it's a nightmare in which I'm trying to get paid.

Darcy rolls his eyes.

- Very clever.

He pauses, breathes in, looks Conor dead in the eye.

- You think this isn't about freedom of speech. You think this is about money. Power. You think we just write what we write and believe what we believe because we're trying to climb the greasy pole like everyone else. Maybe you should see what life does to you when you have to pay your own way.

On Darcy's shoulder, outside the window, the new Business School looms. Conor stands up to leave.

\-   That's the nightmare.

As he steps out the door, Darcy's caffeinated voice leaps out after him.

\-   D'you want to know why we never had problems with diversity here until now? The honest answer.

\-   Why? says Conor, turning around.

\-   Because we never had any diversity. Ha!

And with that Conor turns his back on the university.

***

\-   Man, you're the hottest thing on Dublin TikTok right now… you're being memed to fuck.[4]

Out of the corner of his eye, Conor sees a happy and bruised face. Oisín.

Conor starts to walk away only for Oisín to follow him down the corridor like an intrigued Doberman.

\-   Okay, Conor, so this is the thing. The numbers have gone crazy since the presentation. Everyone wants to hear your take on your supervisor blacking up.

\-   I'm sorry man.

\-   Why be sorry? They love your metrics.

\-   I don't care about metrics—

\-   But you're connecting really well with frustrated, celibate young males. They think you represent them.

\-   Thanks.

\-   That's just the demographic they're trying to up their numbers w—

\-   Thanks.

———————

[4] Are you not on TikTok? What are you doing here at the end?

- Conor, can't you see? This is gold. There's millions of people unrepresented by the mainstream media. You're reaching them. John Bonnar wants to interview you himself. Ask some questions about your experience with Griesmann.

- Dr Guzmán?

- That's her fake name.

- Well why can't she be who she wants to be?

- Well I'd like to be a great white shark, but I'm a stocks manager from South County Dublin.

And it's true: Oisín has been clear on it since childhood. He really would like to be a great white shark.

As they walk on, Oisín athletically avoids bashing into a 5'2 first-year carrying an Extinction Rebellion tote bag. He spins around 360 degrees then catches up with Conor.

- There's an exciting movement building, Conor. It's correcting the overreach of places like this, of people like Griesmann.

- And you think you'll make a load of money.

- Yeah. We will. And what's wrong with that?

- I'm not interested.

- Here, I need to piss man. Let's talk in the bathroom.

- I don't need to piss, Oisín. Actually I really need to talk to my dad. Listen...

Conor stops for a second as a student walks between them down the stairs. The hustle and bustle surrounds them as Oisín stops too. Then the noise thins out and Conor speaks.

- ...You don't like woke? Political correctness?

- Of course not, says Oisín.

- What are you gonna replace it with?

- What?

- How are you gonna talk about race and gender and everything without going back to—

- Listen. There's an untapped market of people who don't like how authoritarian things are becoming. The fact is that institutions are too scared to air these opinions for fear of being cancelled, and all we want to do is sidestep that using online media. This is an amazing opportunity to save free speech, and make a load of money doing—

    - There you go. Money, money, money.

    - Everything's about money.

They stumble down the stairs and into the big brutalist atrium. They're heading towards the door that opens out onto Campus Square.

    - I'm sorry, Oisín. I don't want to be part of this, especially not right now okay? It's exactly a year since my mum died. I don't want to be part of anything today. I just wanna call my dad.

Conor pauses by the door as the light of day hits their faces.

    - Oh fuck, says Oisín. I had no idea. Shit shit shit.

    - It's alright. I'll talk to you soon.

    - No—

Conor's glad to finally be rid of him as he opens the door. He walks out onto Campus Square and straight into a crowd of cheering protestors holding anti-woke placards. They break into spontaneous applause at the sight of him. Oh.

***

Before Conor can register what's going on, a hand slaps into his shoulder in the manner of an over-friendly uncle. John Bonnar.

Already they're several snaps into an unsolicited photo shoot, with dozens of unhealthy-looking men cheering them on from around the Square. Bonnar quickly ushers him up a temporary stage and, trotting over to join, Oisín mouths 'shite' to Conor in apology.

    - Excuse me, ladies and gentlemen, says Bonnar, standing on a soapbox…

He's all projected voice: a shouted complaint of a man, a personified whinge.

- ...I am here today to say no to woke, to protect the integrity of free speech on campus, to illustrate the lengths to which many will go to shut us down.

- G'warn Falmouth!

The shout in the crowd comes from a Dublin accent. The guy looks like one of the university doormen, Conor thinks. One of Bonnar's suits confronts the man and tells him that Mr Bonnar prefers his former career not to be mentioned.

- And I have with me someone who can truly illustrate that...

Conor looks at his watch. He really needs to get away; call his dad. Somehow he feels like he's closing in on some kind of catharsis. It's true that he hasn't figured out what he wants to do with his life, but he has figured out what he doesn't want to do. Live out his father's dreams, for example. Preach to people. Join a cult.

- ...Someone who has been hounded and persecuted for daring to air a free opinion. It's my pleasure to introduce...

After last time he won't make the same mistake twice. There's a lot he could say if he wanted to, but does he want to? — it seems to him that all this was a colossal mistake.

Conor has his first good idea in months. He steps off the stage and, stepping round the sad-looking men, begins to run away. He runs as fast as he can.

- ... Conor Crowley! says Bonnar, as the crowd falls silent.

- We want to hear you, Falmouth, says the same Dublin voice.

- Yep, says Bonnar. The show ended half a decade ago.

- Case closed! says the voice again.

The crowd remains silent as Bonnar begins to twitch impatiently. His breathing gets shallower and his features squirm around his face until finally he cracks.

- I'm not Falmouth Smart, he shouts. I'm not a bloody detective! I'm a *broadcaster*!

Conor turns back to look at the scene. His eyes meet Oisín, who grimaces as if to say sorry for the whole thing. Returning the gesture, Conor heads for the exit.

Oisín, on the other hand, puts his mind to work. There's no point letting yourself get downhearted, he thinks. You've got to take the rough with the smooth and the key to success is treating yourself well after a failure.

So what's for dinner tonight? he asks himself. Not takeaway. Now's the time to be healthy — to bounce back stronger tomorrow. The machine needs fuel. So what should he make? He has potatoes in the house. His mind circles the question then, like a bird of prey, swoops down and plucks the answer out of thin air. Of course, he thinks. The answer was staring at him this whole time. Steak and chips. Superb.

***

A weak ray of sunlight creeps onto St. Stephen's Green. It makes a silly little rainbow in the water fountain where some kids are playing. Meanwhile, the seagulls stare with murderous intent at the office workers eating their sandwiches. Hordes of lonely suits scroll through their phones. An old lady on one of the benches is the only adult who doesn't have a device in her hand, including Conor.

He's been scrolling a while now, creatively inventing reasons not to call his dad. But now he comes across a picture of himself — a thumbnail of him looking angry while Dr Guzmán looks on aghast from the corner. So there it is: 'Student SLAMS down race faking SJW professor in front of crowd.' He notices how unkind he looks in the thumbnail.

That's enough of a shudder for him to put his attention back on to the phone call. Time to call Dad. But just as he's about to suck in his gut and call the old bastard, his phone buzzes. Peter Crowley's got there first.

   - Hi Dad. How are you? Conor says as he picks up the call.

- I'm well, son. I'm well. How are you?
- I'm well too.
- Good. Good. Considering the day…
- Yeah. Exactly.

There's a pause.

- Well, I've, uh, heard about some of the scrapes you've been getting into. Much like your dad. Are you okay?
- I'm okay.
- Your tutor was pretending to be… I'm sorry if I get the wrong one now. Not coloured?
- People of colour, you're supposed to say. But I'm not gonna cancel you Dad, don't worry.
- Well that's a relief. So she was pretending to be people of coloured.
- Well… kind of.
- I should really know anyway, says Peter. They've said they're decolonising the English Department here, you know. I need to make sure there's still space for old Lawrence Sterne.

Conor inhales.

- That's part of what I want to talk about, Dad. I, uh——— I don't really want to be an academic anymore.
- Right.
- This whole thing with Dr Guzmán—
- Come on, son, it's not you that was living a lie.
- That's just half of it, though. There's loads of other reasons I don't want to.
- Like?

It's a struggle to think. He's always found it impossible to explain himself to his dad. Usually, he's so worried about how it will sound that he starts questioning himself before he's even finished the sentence. So he takes time before he speaks.

- I don't want to go around telling people what's right and wrong, and that's what everyone seems to want me to do. I can't stand moral purists and I can't stand cynics either. It seems like everyone is one or the other.

- But you've prospects here. You've worked so—
- I don't know, dad, I can't—
- You can't just drift around like a romantic son. You need prospects, a career—
- But this isn't one. It's—
- How else are you gonna get through this? How are you going to make a living?
- I'll pull pints all my life if I have to.
- I don't want that life for you. I don't want you to have to… ah, bollocks.

He sighs, breathes heavily for a moment, then speaks again.

- You know I wish your mother was here. I'm not the best at talking about this kind of thing.
- I'm not either.

Conor hears his dad composing himself.

- If that's how you feel, son, that that's how you feel. I know that you don't want to live my life. You'll be a loss to the republic of letters, that's all I'm saying.
- Come on Dad. The republic of letters might be better off with a few less PhDs in it.
- Well, you're not completely wrong about that. I hope you give me a call soon to let me know what your plans are at least.
- I will.
- Is there, uh, anything else you want to talk about?
- No, I mean, I guess not.
- Okay then. I suppose I should be g—
- Wait. I mean. Actually… I just wanna say… I wish Mum was here too.
- I know you do, son. Of course you do. She'd be proud of you, though. You know how to stand up for yourself, Conor.

Do I? Conor thinks.

- Thanks, he says.
- I can't believe it's been a year, says his dad. Time—

- Flies, right?

- I was going to say 'is a cunt,' but I suppose you've grasped the point.

- Thank you Dad. I… uh… well you know I love you?

- I… of course. Love you too, son. I'll, uh, call you in a few days.

- Great.

- Good… Bye now.

- Bye.

- Bye.

- Bye.

- Bye bye.

Conor takes a moment to gather himself. He realizes that he hasn't uttered those three words in a whole year. Exactly a year.

Then a ping from his phone arrests his thoughts. He looks down. Katie. He reads it all at once like he's coming up for air.

Hey Conor, I've seen that video you're in. I just wanted to say I think this alt-right thing you're doing is really awful. Your teacher's obviously not okay but exploiting that for views is just wrong.

He considers texting straight away, protesting to her that he's been framed and all of this is just bullshit piled up against him. But he doesn't. Instead he reaches for the phone and texts his dad.

Thanks for the call. Don't worry, I'll work just as hard as ever and I'll do something worthwhile. I've learnt a lot this week, I think. And I'm trying. I'm really trying.

Our handsome hero breathes a sigh of relief and looks out at the park. The old lady smiling pleasantly. The office workers too busy to see their own misery. The little kids playing like it's the most important thing in the world. He sends the message.

Conor is trying. He really is.

Parking Meters

Author's Note: This story takes place before the events of Mister Professor, when Oisín and Conor shared a house as undergraduates.

- My keys, Oisín. Have you seen them?

- Bitcoin's up again. Bro, I've been pumping so long I'm not sure I'll even need to take a dump.

- I had them last night in the pub, before you left and brought your mates from Business round here. I'm sure they were out on the table.

- Sorry, bro, haven't seen them. I blacked out after we left Diceys.

- I swear they were on the table, Conor says. I swear.

Our handsome hero rushes through his Dublin house-share. He is Conor Crowley, he is looking for his keys, and he is — as he tells his smooth-tongued housemate, Oisín — completely in control of the situation.

- I'm completely in control of the situation, alright?, he says, unconvincingly.

Conor's runners clatter against the hardwood floor. Down and up he paces like a pigeon stuck in a hall of mirrors. It's the hottest day of the year and, even as morning trickles into afternoon, the heat is beginning to stifle.

- Just give me a break, he says.

- The break, bro, has been given, Oisín says. And it has turned into a dirty weekend away from the kids. You said this would take one minute.

Oisín sits down. The fact is that a sledgehammer is pounding against his forehead every time his heart beats. It is not pretty. But his hangovers never are.

- They're somewhere here, alright? says Conor. Maybe if you helped me look for them—

- We'd both waste our time?

- Well you and your Business Studies mates were in this room last night, weren't you?

- I'm sorry, bro, I really am. But listen... this is making my hangover hit way harder. I just need to get out and—

- Couldn't you clean the flat or something? Conor asks. What did you do last night? Why is there olive oil on the floor?

- That must've been Steve. His mum's Greek.

- So?

- They use a lot of olive oil.

- What about the cans of Pratzky all over the place?

- His dad's Czech.

- And?

- Well he's adopted, so maybe he has identity issues. Ah, Jesus bro, my head. I don't know...There's this little game he likes to play sometimes. I...

God's sunlight seeps in through the window, and it is not at all welcome.

- ...aaaaaaaaaaah. My head is in bits, says Oisín.

- Well perhaps next time he's here, Conor says, he could refrain from performing the traditional folk games of his people.

- Conor, can't we just go? If I don't go out and take on this hangover I'm going to spend my day sinking into despair...

From the squalor of the sofa, Oisín raises a Christlike hand.

- ...Conor, I get it. I'm sorry. I understand your frustration. I can't remember what happened to your keys, but I wouldn't let anyone mess with them, I swear. They'll be around here somewhere sure.

And like Christ, he receives no mercy.

- Move over — I need to look under that cushion.

- Conor, can we please go? I have keys. I cannot stress to you how much anguish this hangover is causing me. I have to leave the house now… or… or I may never leave again.

- Move over — I need to look under that cushion, Conor repeats.

- I know you don't wanna hear this — I get it. But I must stress that this anguish is not just physical. It has taken on a metaphysical dimension.

- Move over.

- You looked under that cushion a second ago.

- I know I did.

- Which begs the question: why are you looking there again?

- Fuck up!

Wily Oisín flings himself from the sofa. He grabs his car keys, twirls them, and congratulates himself on rising above Conor's hostility. There is no money to be made, he tells himself, in being angry.

- Okay, bro. You can stay here all day if you like but I'm getting in the car.

- Wait, we're not driving are we? asks stress-laden Conor.

- Yeah. Why?

- We can't drive — the protest is in town.

- Don't worry about that, the Drury Street car park always has spaces.

- No, I mean, it'll look terrible. You can't drive to a climate change protest.

- Why not?

- Because they're protesting about climate change.

- So?

- So you can't drive, man.

- Why?

- Because it's a climate change protest.

Wily Oisín pauses and considers.

- Are you aware of something called circular logic, bro? he asks.

- It's a climate change protest!

- I see.

The last cushion left alive flutters through the air following a strong scoop from stress-laden Conor. Then Oisín says

- I can see you're stressed, bro, but all the evidence suggests it will be fine. Katie's coming later on for one thing.

- So?

- So she won't see you when we're driving. And you're only going because you want to impress her.

- What? That's not true.

- So you're going because of a passionate commitment to the climate?

- Well you're only going because you want to shift Karla—

- And because I need to fill the time before me and Steve go for a drink.

- Who is this Steve anyway? You and him are getting through a lot of alcohol and lubricant together.

- Steve Novak. He's one of the lads from my course. We were on the KPMG internship together and he arranged pints for tonight, but I can't have him meet Karla. She already finds it hard to like me because she's apparently 'against global capitalism.' And Stevey is a walking woke bomb.

Conor gestures to the door.

- Alright man let's go. But you've got to stop saying 'woke'. You sound like a middle-market newspaper.

- I have found no other satisfactory, language, bro. Plus I study Business. Analysis is what I do.

II

   - D'ye have any codeine? asks thoughtful Oisín.

   - Codeine? Conor asks. Christ, can't you take a paracetamol?

   - My condition calls for something more severe.

   - It's difficult to pity you, Conor says.

Oisín's anguish makes itself visible.

   - Okay, I've got ibuprofen. It's in my backpack, says Conor. I think I left a Lucozade in there too. You can have it. Just take the whole bag.

   - You soothe my anguish, Conor.

So speaks smooth-tongued Oisín as the two friends walk to the expectant Opel Corsa. Lying out there in the heat, still shiny from the showroom with door handles hot to the touch, it gleams a wine-dark shade of blue only rarely found lapping up Irish shores.

   - What colour is it again?

   - Wine-dark sea blue, says Oisín proudly.

   - So it's blue.

   - The colour of the Mediterranean Sea.

   - It's nice though, it really is. For a Vauxhall Corsa. How's the AC?

Oisín gapes at the new car.

   - There is nothing that can trouble the air conditioning technology of the 2015 Opel Corsa, he says. Nothing in all Europe…

He pauses and considers.

   - …And say *Opel* Corsa. You're in Ireland.

Five minutes later and they're both panting like dogs in a sauna. Towards the horizon there is a line of cars broken only by young lads on pedal bikes who pull wheelies in political protest. When Dublin reaches thirty centigrade, apocalypse is a part of life. It's just what happens when the government considers public transport a decadence. There's nothing else to it.

Horns sound close by and Conor sticks his head out the window. He sees nothing at all and his only sense enriched is smell. Thick bubbles fizzing in the air lashed with malt and suncream on skin.

- Man, I need a cool breeze, says Conor.

- You know, bro, I can't believe you said Vauxhall just then. I knew you were English, but not that English.

- It's just where I grew up, man. Three of my grandparents are Irish.

- Vauxhall, Conor? *Vauxhall?* I have to say, Conor: it smacks of colonisation.

- My great-grandad was in the 'Ra, man.

- I thought you said he was on the British side.

- Oisín, how could he be on the British side if he was in the 'Ra?

- You said he fought for the British in the war.

- In World War One, yeah, then he joined the 'Ra.

- So he was on the British side.

Thoughtful Oisín turns the radio down. The DJ prophesies that Dublin's highest ever temperature will be clocked this afternoon. An advert for a mattress company plays and Oisín's smile thickens.

When the advert ends, Oisín turns the radio off and looks at Conor honestly. With brotherly affection, he says

- You're right though, bro. We could definitely do with a breeze.

III

Crumbling tarmac washes them to the Drury Street car park like the ferryman over the dark Styx. The water in their bottles is hot. Conor sweats social anxiety.

They reach South William Street as the first protestors trickle through the grey streets like water between rocks, twinkling with tanning oil. They are only a hint of the hordes to come — scouts for a conquering army still yet to show.

Just stragglers, thinks Conor: no sight of Karla or Katie.

There is a taste of something delicious in the air, a half note of pheromones flickering off bodies in the hazy early afternoon. They linger there then meld with smells from bins and hot lost malt drifting over from the Guinness factory, made stronger by summer.

- Do you smell that? asks Oisín.
- Coffee?
- Malt.
- Are you sure? This far into town?
- You can always smell Dublin in the sun, bro. Even on South William Street. It's just buried beneath all that pretentious coffee.

With a crackle of hot tarmac the Corsa gets through the marchers to Drury Street, enclosed tightly by parked cars on its two sides. Pubs and shit shops selling fake Irish culture loom above them in the firing sun like gallows.

Then Conor sees that the car park's closed — closed!

- I thought you said Drury Street was open, Oisín? Christ, they'll be here soon and they'll see us. Driving to a climate change protest — I warned you! I warned you!

Oisín pauses, considers.

- We'll get to one of the backroads by Pearse Street. There's a spot I can call in a favour. Erne Place.
- But then we have to drive through the protest.
- And?
- No, no, noooooooooooooooooooo man. What if the protestors see us?
- So what? They're not gonna lynch us.
- That's exactly the type of thing people say before they get lynched.

IV

They turn onto the north of Stephen's Green and into the fire. Here the army is innumerate. Like penitent religious warriors they strain through pavement, spilling down the road when their path vanishes and angling themselves shadewards when the beating sun burns too hot.

Strange visions whizz into Conor's head. Flagellants with medieval shame, who nonetheless regard their doubters as more shameful for doubting. Then his vision is interrupted by two girls walking towards him and thoughtful Oisín with great fury painted in their eyes.

Karla — Katie!

They are in some kind of argument. Katie leads Karla by her arm out of the crowd like a child from play. Karla's whine is raucous enough to be heard by Oisín, who is roused at once.

- Shite! says Oisín. Okay, bro, we've got to hide.

Thoughtful Oisín spins hands hectically until his wheel spits a click at him. He looks desperately for clearings into which the Corsa can squeeze, then clunks it onto the curb as they speed off with a shrill screech which sparks jeers from the crowd. They can't get through though: each gap between the protestors closes just as quickly as it opens.

The girls are edging closer. Though they can't see the car yet, they soon will — a thought which plunges stress-laden Conor into a desperate and fear-tinged shout.

- What now? What now?

- Plan B. Open the glovebox.

Our handsome hero does what he is told. He clicks open the glovebox and is met with two terrible sights. Blood red and block-capitalled, two baseball caps emblazoned with the slogan

MAKE AMERICA GREAT AGAIN

- Trust me, Conor, this has saved me so many times.

Conor looks like he's just received a surprisingly efficient disembowelment.

- You mean you carry these around with you? Not one but two?

- Three, says Oisín. Jesus, that's Karla right there. Put it on — quick!

Conor's about to drop the hats in horror when Oisín clutches them and puts one on Conor's head. Then the hat is on his head too and the Corsa is in first and Oisín is accelerating with as much speed as his floor-bound foot can muster. The protestors spring out the way with scattered screams. As they whizz through, Conor thinks he sees Katie looking at him in great shock, then they skir round the corner and she vanishes. They take one backstreet, then another, and speedily reach a lane squeezed between the back of a mattress shop and some council flats.

They're about to smash into a redbrick wall when Oisín slams the breaks, nearly triggering the airbags. Suddenly there is silence on the dark, hot tarmac.

Conor looks around. On the right: a seagull perched in front of the flats. On the left: a parking meter. Above: blue sky scorched pale by the burning sun. The sound of children playing comes from the distance.

Conor and Oisín look at each other. Take off the two hats. Resume breathing.

- Lucky that, says Oisín.

- Lucky?

- We're in our parking spot.

V

- Hold on, bro, Oisín says, I just need to check my cryptocurrency.

Our handsome hero takes a quick breath in and waits for Oisín to check.

- Shit, Oisín, what are we gonna do? Even if they didn't see our faces, they'll recognize us from our tops.

- D'ye reckon I could open that Lucozade bro?

Wily Oisín claws through Conor's rucksack looking for the bottle. Conor looks on impatiently. Protestors trickle by the lane.

Further up Pearse Street, marching beats thump towards them with protesting yelps and murderous intent. Sounds of slogans bleat then bounce with resonating treble all the way onto Erne Place Lower.

As the bag jangles, Oisín finally produces the Lucozade. He unscrews the lid and joyfully sucks in the gurgling bubbles, popping another ibuprofen as he does so.

- Can we be quick please? asks Conor. They're gonna catch us.

- You know, bro. I've never had a Lucozade which didn't cure my hangover.

- Oisín? Can we be quick? says Conor, as two men drunk on oat milk lattes glide past the alley.

- Let's be slow, bro. Take as much time as we need. I've got a plan.

Pointing towards a red fire door strewn with crisp packets, wily Oisín gets out of the car. Conor, meanwhile, looks at him fearfully. It's only five quick seconds before kind Conor hears murmurs through Oisín's phone — murmurs which sound strangely like somebody saying 'no bother at all.'

- Mick says no bother at all, Oisín grins.

- Mick?

- Yeah, Mattress Mick.

- What?

- You're telling me you don't know Mattress Mick?

- No. But what's he gonna do? Sell us a mattress?

- Wow, you really are English. Mick's not just a mattress seller. He's Ireland's biggest wholesaler. Harnesses, sports equipment, liquified natural g—

- Which would be great if we were setting up a JD Sports, but—

- Don't you see Conor? He's got a whole shipment of Ireland rugby jerseys come in from China this morning…

Oisín looks admiringly into the middle distance.

- …Neat little money spinner this close to the Aviva, he says.

- And?

- We go into the mattress shop through the back door, change our tops, then go out the front. Nobody will recognise us and nobody will see the car.

- I'm not sure a climate change protest is going to be chock-a-block with rugby fans, Oisín. It's July.

- Listen, I've thought about this. There's a Sharpie in the Corsa. We add some climate change slogans to the Ireland jerseys and it just looks like we're putting our own spin on the whole protest fashion. That's what the climate change people will think.

- They'll think we're a particularly unimaginative set of undercover Gardaí, Oisín.

- Come on, man. You think everyone here isn't thinking up their best costume for the show?

Our handsome hero lets it run through his head. Maybe it could work? They just have to avoid getting killed, not become the protestors' best friends.

- Okay, man, let's do it. Fuck it.

- Yes, bro! Now while I'm in your good books, I'm gonna have to break some bad news.

Kind Conor looks at Oisín knowingly, ready for the worst.

- Oh come on, bro, don't look at me like that. I'm not a fucking paedophile.

- Not that I know of.

- Your keys are in your rucksack.

Now Conor looks ready for a suicide attack — like he's keen to kill both of them plus anyone who might be within explosion range. That is until the kind eyes of Oisín look back at him poignantly.

- I'm sorry bro. I must've left them in your bag once the games started last night. I'll make it up to you, I promise. And I know I've not been good enough cleaning lately. I'll make that up to you too. I'll buy you a pint. I'll buy you two pints.

- Man, it's not always about pints.

Wily Oisín's eyes give the impression that he doesn't agree.

- Alright, I'll pay the parking meter as well.

- Mate, it doesn't matter. All things considered it's quite a touching gesture. You know, that you put the keys in the bag... since you were blackout drunk and everything. Let's just... let's go get changed.

VI

Eight minutes later and they're stepping through Mick's front door, their odd outfits the only thing marking any difference from the vegan crowd.

Conor's green Ireland jersey says

Tackle Climate Change!

Oisín's says

Kick Climate Change Into Touch!

Thought-quick Oisín grins proudly as though a revitalising breeze whisks through his hair. Odd, because in the throbbing sun, there's no wind this side of the Atlantic Ocean. Near them, marching, the crowd swells.

Down towards Ringsend, a stage is being built. Feedback from the microphone whirls and swirls through the street at incredible volume as a mass of bodies lumbers towards it.

- But why can't we just go home? asks stress-laden Conor.

His palms are sweaty. Even sweatier than normal.

- Because going home would just make us look weird, replies Oisín.

- I'm feeling a bit fucked, man.

- Come on, bro. Courage. You're not fucked. If anything, you're unfucked. Listen, bro...

He freezes them both in the middle of the crowd and puts his hand on Conor's shoulder. Protestors pass them by like a current past a pontoon.

- ...If you're right, and you did catch Katie's eye, then she's probably wondering right now whether it was us. If we suddenly cancel our plans with them, all we do is confirm this suspicion.

- I don't know man.

- I'm telling you, bro, you're unfucked.

- Am I though? I don't feel unfucked.

- Unfuck yourself then, says Oisin, looking him in the eye. You know why?

- Why?

- Because that's them there.

Waving under the sun is a bright-eyed girl with a cool smile. Next to her stands flame-haired a companion, huffing in the fearful sun. One of them is Irish; the other English. One calm and collected; the other sharp and stressed.

Bright-eyed Katie leads while Karla trudges behind on mopey feet. Sidestepping through the sweat-strewn red bodies, Katie raises her voice and says, in a faint Meath accent

- You won't believe what we just saw, lads...

They stop halfway across the road as a strange look comes onto thoughtful Conor's face. He looks much like a Tory MP caught with a special lady somewhere that he shouldn't be. A bush, perhaps.

- …Some lads in Make America Great Again hats nearly ran us down. They looked like they were trying to scare the protestors. Some protestors chased after them but they were long gone by then.

- A mob? says Conor.

- Protestors, yeah. It was crazy.

Flame-haired Karla enters the conversation certainly. Her voice is crisp, curt, and confidently North London.

- They were terrorists. They could've been terrorists. Incel terrorists.

- Surely not incels, says Oisín. Maybe terrorists, but not virgins.

- D—, did you see what they were driving? asks Conor.

- It was a little hatchback, says Katie. Purple, I think.

- I think I saw that. But it wasn't purple — it was Wine-Dark Ocean Blue, Oisín interjects.

- We didn't see anyone wearing MAGA hats, says Conor.

- Not that I saw, says Oisín. I didn't see any incels, either.

- We didn't see who was inside, Conor interrupts. He and Oisín look at each other.

They're all still for a while as Conor notices that Oisín's eyes are hovering on Karla's face. His stare makes it all too clear that she's crucial to him: he looks at her like he's sunk in love.

Which is mad, thinks Conor with a cold sigh — *she's* got her stare fixed over the road where the glistening backs of the crowd congregate, sweating. They lurch towards the stage like migrating animals.

- I think she's about to come on, says Karla. They're just doing the sound check.
- She? says Oisín.
- Gina Kelly. She's an environmental lawyer. The key speaker today and Katie's doing an internship with her. She's amazing.

Katie blushes. So does Oisín.

- She's really not that great, Katie says.

From the hazy air comes the big broad boom of subwoofers, trembling with hard bass notes that bounce off the buildings then down through the hot air and into the vibrating crowd, which cheers in joy.

Prancing around the pulpit antelope-like is a white-shirted woman, fortyish with short hair and an infectious air of confidence. She's greeted by wild applause.

- Is that her?

Shards of excitement glint off the eyes of headstrong Karla, who smiles.

- That's her. Did you hear her on Gerry Adams' sustainability podcast? she asks Katie.
- That's one of my favourites, says Oisín to Karla.

Conor balks at him.

But Karla's in her own world. Silent and spellbound, she mouths to herself

- God, Gina looks beautiful.

The crowd spews noise like lava from a volcano. Gina Kelly speaks.

- Hellooooooooooooooooooooooooooooooooooooooo Dublin!

Cheers ring out like sirens in the street. Gina Kelly is loved.

- We have been fighting for the environmental movement for twenty years. In the law, in the media, and in the political arena. And I must tell you, my friends, that we have achieved nothing! Twenty years ago our rivers were thick with fat, our fish were dying, and the politicians were ignoring everything we said. Today none those problems are better — all are catastrophically worse. So we must keep doing what we are doing!

Shrill shouts.

- We have to end fossil fuels. We have to slow down energy use, stop intensive farming. We have to stop the exploitation of our rainforests abroad and the destruction of our seas and rivers at home. We have to dismantle systemic racism and stand with the LGBTQIA+ community. Most importantly, we have to destroy all forms of oppressive power and create a society which is based not on privilege but on equality for all humans and all animals. We have to do this within fifteen years or face extinction not just for ourselves, but for all life on earth. Can we do it?

No, thinks Conor.

- You, the people of Dublin — the people of the world — will decide that!

Thick like gravy the noise gloops from the mass of bodies watching her. With the inspiring talk over, she strolls off the stage like a preacher, highfiving each protestor who needs her. They want her redemption, sticking out their hands greedily like lepers stretching for their saviour.

- Well that was stupid, says Oisín.

The next speaker starts as they walk away from the stage. He advertises some slam poetry, which is coming up soon.

- Let's get out of here before that starts, says Oisín, shaken. He's ignored.

- She's so inspirational, says Karla. It's amazing you've got an internship with her.

- Yeah, replies thoughtful Katie. The internship isn't that great though. There's a lot of people there, but Gina's a little… visionary.

- That's a good thing, says Karla.

- Well, yeah, but sometimes it gets in the way of what you're actually doing. Like there was this Zoom call the week after George Floyd died. She joined looking incredibly traumatized and made everyone stop talking. Then she stood up on her desk and made a speech about what she was doing *personally* to combat systemic racism. She kept saying that — *personally*. Like she could solve the problem herself. Plus talking about how much she loves Nina Simone, as if that was relevant.

- I love Nina Simone, says Karla.

Someone's phone pings. Our handsome hero checks his and gets nothing. Brave Karla checks hers too and is somehow offended it's not hers.

- That's her now, says Katie. She's texting me to come to the office for an impromptu mind mapping session. Says it's urgent. She's always doing this.

- You better go, says Karla with a concerned look.

- Sure, I spose I should. It could be a few hours, sorry. And she's gone.

- So, says Karla, do you guys want to see some slam poetry while we're waiting for Katie?

Death crawls up Oisín's face and into his eyes.

VII

- I thought it was… okay, says Conor, fifty-five minutes later, nauseous from the slam poetry.

- What about you? asks Karla, interrogating.

- I'm not sure, says Oisín, halfway through I got lost in this dream of moving to America and joining the Republican Party.

- Like I completely agree with you… with…. it, Conor says to Karla. And I get that he was making a point—

- About plastic pollution? Oisín interjects. It wasn't a point I felt needed to be made through slam poetry.

Headstrong Karla looks on and says

- She's standing up for something. I think that's amazing. And I think it was a great poem.

Oisín breathes heavily.

- Standing up for what? Getting rid of plastic? Amazing. She makes Martin Luther King look like Dustin the Turkey sure.

Thought-quick Oisín points over the road to a pubic-hair-heavy couple. They drink something tasty out of an old Colman's mustard jar.

- You think your hairy armpits are gonna save the world?

- I think it's worthwhile to stand up for something that's important, says flame-haired Karla.

- Yeah, everyone wants to feel important.

- It *is* important. Climate change is literally killing people.

- So there's a problem. But it's not gonna be solved by slam poetry.

- Everyone has to do their bit. It spreads awareness, which is one of the most important things. What doesn't help is being cynical about it.

Wily Oisín locks eyes with Karla angrily, yet romantically, until Conor breaks it up.

- I think if everyone could just sit down and discuss it, says Conor, then the problem would be a lot easier to deal with.

They both look at him like he's just suggested they all get naked.

- How can you sit down and discuss something with people who think the world's about to end? says Oisín.

- How can you sit down and discuss something when the world *is* about to end? says Karla.

- Um, says Conor.

Karla speaks:

- Nothing has ever gotten better by people sitting around being dicks, Oisín.

- What are you trying to say? Oisín replies. Look at your wan. What's Gina Kelly doing to make the world better? Going around trying to be a visionary intellectual, dining out on all the young followers she has. Lapping up adulation like she's a hero. Isn't that pathetic?

- She's using her skills to save the world—

- And have people cheer her.

- She deserves to be cheered. She's helping to save the world. She's doing a lot more than you are walking around in a rugby shirt.

Brave Karla looks into his eyes full of disdain as Oisín teeters through his words like a little rascal caught stealing boiled sweets.

- You like her, don't you? You think she's... attractive.

- What good is it doing writing slogans on a rugby shirt?

- But don't you think... the adulation... She's so sanctimonious!

- I think she's great.

- I...

But the power has fled Oisín's speech. Kind Conor looks on, concerned.

- Maybe we should talk about something else, says Conor.

- So sanctimonious! says Oisín.

- She's doing some good, Oisín, says Karla. That's incredibly attractive. Going around being a dick about it is incredibly *unattractive*.

Knocked-back and punch-drunk, thought-quick Oisín lets pride take over him.

- Yeah well... She's not gonna change the world. She's just one person. And anyway... the world is great. None of you people appreciate that we have the highest living standards in history... and that didn't come about because we're all so irredeemably racist and sexist and committing genocide against the natural world. I don't know why you like her so much.

- I like people who fight injustice — activists, artists. Not stupid lads who have to make everything about rugby!

She stares at his shirt with cruel eyes. The shirt looks back at her and says with kind and simple sincerity ***Kick Climate Change into Touch!***

- You just want to be part of something, says Oisín.
- You just want money.
- She's the one making a living off climate change.
- You're just jealous.
- And why would I be jealous of her?
- Because the people think she's gorgeous for doing what's right.
- Who cares about 'the people'?
- Because I think she's gorgeous!
- I need to go. I— I have to… check my cryptocurrency.

Wily Oisín slips out without speaking any more rash words.

- Good, she shouts after him. I don't need to be seen with any more bloody rugby fans!

He's gone though, which leaves Karla with Conor and Conor looking for an excuse to leave. Her eyes turn to his jersey, which says earnestly

Tackle Climate Change!

The eyes are hot with disgust.

- I'm sorry if Oisín and me, um, overstepped the mark back there, says Conor.
- You? You'd be too afraid to even look at the mark, Conor.

She looks over his head like he's a junkie begging drug money.

- I'm going into the shop, she says. You wait outside.

Brave Karla, flame-haired, marches through the close-packed crowd like a soldier. Into Londis she goes.

Wait, thinks our handsome hero… does she mean I'm not allowed? That seems to be what's going on: some subtle game that's being played. He's not really sure why he isn't allowed in — not even really sure *that* he isn't allowed in, but he's not in any mood for testing whichever dumb theory his brain might stupidly produce. It's best that Karla makes up his mind for him: she knows what's best.

Yet something still nags. Can he not just, like, leave? When was it that he decided to give up control of his will like this? When did he wake up and start letting friends tell him what to do? Karla… Oisín.

Fuck it! He thinks. He's off. Time for a trip to the pub. Turning his back on the warm evening sun, his feet find rhythm and he begins to escape it all.

- Conor!

A shout.

- Where are you going?

It's Karla.

- Nowhere.

That's right, he thinks. He's going nowhere at all.

- I saw something amazing in Londis, says Karla.
- In Londis? replies Conor.
- Central Cee is in there.
- What?
- Central Cee.
- The rapper?
- Yeah.
- In Londis?
- Yeah!
- Are you sure?
- Conor, rappers go to Londis too.
- Wouldn't he be somewhere more expensive?
- Not if he remembers his roots, she says seriously.

Come on, I'm gonna ask for a picture.

Her eyes roll contemptuously as she gestures for him to follow her in. Kind Conor does so obediently, then sets eyes on Central Cee — and...

It's not him. That's not all though, for not only is this guy not Mr Cee — he doesn't look anything like him. Not a single tattoo, no hip hop fashion: just chinos, boat shoes, and brown skin.

- Wish me luck, whispers Karla.

I've got to tell her, Conor thinks. I've got to tell her. Well, without offending her.

- Karla! He whispers.
- What?

She's only four steps from the guy — four steps from idiocy — and that's far too close for Conor to say anything to her without him hearing.

- Sorry, um... that's not—
- He's about to check out, she hisses.
- It's not, he whispers... it's not him.
- Shhhhh. I'm going over.

That's when the choice makes itself clear. Either stay in the shop and die or cut clean and leave at last. Conor thinks: he should have done this a long, long time ago. And so he turns his back, ready to get out quickly.

Then he picks his pace up to a run. Exiting Londis, he runs through the seagulls and the rubbish with the sun finally falling below the buildings behind him. He runs onto Grafton Street past a busker playing Japanese folk music in English and German and then onto Wicklow Street past nothing interesting at all.

The endorphins kick in. The late-day heat warms his back as his feet pound the cobbles on South William Street. Now the endorphins are fizzing in his head and pumping down his veins to his hands and feet. Blood pumps and pumps and

- Conor!

A shout. Again. Conor turns around.

But this time it's not Karla. Instead, a bright-eyed girl is sitting on some steps with flowers for sale behind her. She holds her hand to her brow to keep the fading sunlight from dazzling her eyes and looks at him pensively as people rush by her head.

- Nice run?
- Oh, hey Katie… yeah… I was just… you know how it is.

She smiles as she gestures for him to take a seat by her.

- So why are you running? she asks.
- Ah, I… can I tell you later?
- Sure.
- So… what are you doing on the Powerscourt steps? Conor says.
- Well… can I tell you later?
- Oh, okay.

Katie lets silence cut into the conversation. Then she looks back at Conor and catches his quick eye.

- Is everything okay? he says.
- I could ask you the same question.
- How's Mummy Climate Change?
- Gina? Oh, she's grand.
- Yeah?
- Well, actually she's an arsehole. She made a pass at me. She's really creepy.
- Like… she tried to kiss you?
- Well yeah.
- Oh shit, I'm sorry. Are you okay?
- I mean… yeah, I guess.
- Do you mean it was like… assault?

Out of nowhere, tears fill up her eyes and run down her flushed cheeks.

- I… I just feel really awful. It was this little office and she got really close to me and then asked if she could kiss me. She was up so close I could see her teeth, and I said no and I left, and… I've been here by myself for half an hour because I didn't want to talk to anyone.

- Shit, says Conor. I'm sorry.

- I'm just angry because I'm… I'm working really hard to be something good, doing all the work, like. And she probably just thinks I'm some dumb intern she can…

- Yeah. She's a bit of a cult leader, Katie.

Out of the fading sky swoops a fierce-eyed seagull with a paper wrapper clasped in its beak. It begins to squall as it flies over Katie and Conor. Screeching it soars up to the winds, over the last remnants of the crowd and beyond to the dreamlike banks of the black Liffey.

Katie pulls kind Conor close to her, then they hug.

- To be honest, I didn't want to talk to anyone about it…

She pulls back and he sees her smiling.

- …But you were running in the middle of town in an Ireland rugby top which says *TACKLE Climate Change!*

- Karla, Conor says. She saw Central Cee — or thought she did — but it was just a guy whose skin colour looked the same. I tried to tell her but… I don't know. She was kind of hard to talk to.

- Oh my God, says Katie. She did the same thing earlier. I had to drag her away from Stephen's Green because she thought she saw Sandra Oh. It was a Chinese tourist filming the ducks.

- Oof.

- One time she thought she saw Barry Keoghan. This was like two minutes after she stepped onto the Northside. The kid even got her number. She just sees types and can't get them out of her head.

- She can't question her instincts.

- Neither can Oisín, says Katie.

There's a second's pause in which the shouts of the street are all they hear. Two protestors holding cardboard placards walk past into the twilight.

- Will we get a drink? asks Katie.

- Yeah, let's do it. Should we—

- Mmm… let's not invite Karla. She's been acting like a child all day.

- Oisín?

- Oh, God no. I just saw he posted an Instagram story with Steve Novak, this lad I knew in first year. Steve's the most annoyingly laddy lad in the world. He's like all the worst things about rugby encapsulated in one person.

She shows a video of Oisín and a friend downing pints together. The friend wears chinos and boat shoes with a big, gold watch. Christ, thinks our handsome hero. That's the guy who Karla thought was…

Rejjie Snow.

- Did you say you knew this guy in first year? asks Conor.

- Yeah. Steve Novak.

- Oh god.

- Your man used to play this weird game where he'd dribble olive oil on the floor, then, like, put cans of lager—

- He was in Londis. That's who Karla—

- What?

- That's who she thought was Central—

- No way.

- Shit, I'll tell you in the pub.

VIII

Foam spills from Conor's pint onto the varnished brown bar of Grogan's pub. Light falls from the silver chandelier onto dribbles of beer gathered there, making a specular reflection which no one sees. Shouts bounce off the red walls and back into the mouths of the patrons.

- Eleven fifty, says the barman. It's cash only.

- That's grand, says Conor. He brandishes two ten euro notes.

Scrambling away his change, he takes their two pints down to the booth where Katie sits looking at him. He sets them down, smiles.

- Thanks, says Katie.
- How you feeling? he asks.
- A bit bleak.

He sips greedily, taking the cream first then the black stout resting under it like Liffey water beneath a full moon.

- Because of Gina?
- Not even. About the climate. I genuinely don't see how we can get out of it.
- Ah, says Conor, glugging. Sure look. Greta Thunberg will sort it all out.
- No she won't.
- We need a leader then, don't we?
- Well who are these leaders?

Kind Conor half-smiles then forgets it all. His pint tastes good.

- So what d'you think we can do? he asks.
- I don't know.
- I don't know either.
- I mean the reality is that we're all hypocrites, says Katie. How could we not be? Our entire economy is built on it. Like me and Karla drove here today.
- You drove?!
- Yeah, I'm sorry! But the buses are just… shite. Underfunded, overused, you know — that's what it's like in Dublin. Plus the LUAS—
- No… it's fine. We drove as well.
- You did?
- We were in that Opel Corsa. With the… Trump hats.
- What? Are you serious?!
- We didn't want you two to know it was us.

She whips out her phone, brings RTÉ up, and shows him the latest headlines. Bannered at the head of the page in serious font:

FAR-RIGHT DISRUPTION AT CLIMATE CHANGE PROTEST

- **Unidentified Males Drive Dangerously Through Protest in 'MAGA' hats**
- **Gardaí Urge Calm**
- **Suspected Car Impounded After Failing to Pay Parking Meter**

Katie's eyes swell in disbelief as she shakes her head. Conor shrugs.

- Of course, he says. Oisín didn't pay the meter.
- What are you gonna do?
- I reckon another pint, he says.

Outside evening's taken over. The sun dips below the roofs. Heat rises softly as blue sky slowly switches to orange and red.

On Erne Place, a crowd has gathered. They bear iPhones which snap away in the last light. Guards tell them not to move too close as the tow truck grapples a wine-dark Opel Corsa on its back and reverses out of the narrow lane onto Pearse Street. Still in the air is the smell of summer — deathless, dear, and dirty — falling into the Liffey and rising back to the crowd's noses once again, rising to thousand-year-old streets still with air in their lungs.

The only moral I'll offer you people is… well, actually, you can probably guess what I think anyway.

Sad Ones

The Wind and the Rain

The library is cold today. The library is dark today. I sit at my desk, still, as the wind batters the walls outside sounding like it could wake the dead.

People take shelter in here, even as the library's central heating struggles to keep out the chill. I sit above the atrium, overlooking it from my own little vantage point. It's almost full down there, keen first-years mixed with weary-looking graduate students who only come here when the newer part of the library is closed. I like to peer over and evaluate their outfits; usually, the most stylish people look the coldest, which makes sense. I'm an idiot for wearing a dress, I think, as the rain beats rhythmically on the library's roof.

A figure walks past my desk, her footsteps pattering the ground and echoing nicely off the walls. She steps past yellow buckets which are scattered around the floor to catch drips of rain seeping through the roof. The sounds harmonise for a second before they're drowned out by the laughter of lads somewhere on another floor.

I started this morning with the sunniest intentions. I was going to envelop myself in *The Melodramatic Imagination*, note two chapters, then get a nice start on my essay plan after a €12 lunch salad. Now my neck hurts from looking at my phone for hours and there's a gnawing pain in my stomach because it's 17:32 and I haven't eaten and I don't deserve to either. Sometimes stories pop up on my Instagram which show people laughing in the rain on Westmoreland Street or chatting on the Arts Block couches.

These stories are like fresh snow on Christmas morning. There's a promise underneath them, if I can only get to it. I swipe up with my thumb, wait for the wheel to spin, and… nothing. Again. Nothing. Again. New post from Ciara Keogan. Ciara's a girl I knew at school; she was cooler than me and stupider too. She's out with the gals, presumably last weekend. But then she could be out any day of the week, knowing her. I tap the heart on the screen twice. Like.

Hold on. I can hear someone coming towards me. I put my phone down and look at my laptop, which displays a word document: notes I made yesterday, covering my tracks to people walking past. Time for some anonymous typing.

Footsteps. Loud. Masculine footsteps. He's passed now. A beautiful boy. Tall. Beige polo jacket. Doc Martens. I see him a lot here. Once every few days the same girl comes up to his desk and they complain about their tutors. I heard him outside a lecture hall once talking with another boy about how he treats women. Well, he says. They want to be looked after, he says. That's all they want, he says. I was on the sofa opposite him; he didn't see me.

It's been a while for me. Since sex, I mean. It's been too long since I tried to get kissed, even. You have to try. Dicks don't just pop up like adverts – not since I deleted Tinder anyway. And even if they did you wouldn't want it like that. It's not whack-a-mole.

Four months since the last time. Yeah yeah. You remember. Ciaran, the country boy with the Limerick accent. He pushed in the queue outside Doyle's for me and then he bought me a drink and after that I felt like I owed him something. After we finished, he was looking at me, really romantic like, but I called him a culchie as a joke and he looked away, down to his feet. He tried to deflect it, call me a West Brit, act like he wasn't offended. But he was. Upset. I felt like an idiot.

What I should've said was:

'It's alright, I'm a culchie too now. We had to move to Wicklow in my last year of school because my dad lost his business.'

But that's too South Dublin. I should've said:

'I'm a South Dublin girl, hating boggers is part of my cultural heritage.'

To show him I could be ironic about it. That I knew what I was like and that it was okay. But how could I think to say this right thing at the right time?

He didn't say anything nice to me either. Culchie. Christ, you think you can't do any worse than a rugby boy until you meet a GAA boy. And all the others here at Trinity are English and more Nigel Farage than Harry Styles. Remember the one I went to No Name Bar with. He was alright till I took the piss out of Brexit. Thought that was a winner. Nope. Next one will be another guy making me watch Leinster Rugby matches, just like Dad. If there is another one. Remember what Granny said when Mum told her about the divorce. Don't get left on the shelf, that's all.

Facebook Messenger. No notifications. Swipe up. No notifications. Open Gmail. No new emails on **murphyell9@tcd.ie**. Nothing on **ellzbellz1998@gmail.com** either. Instagram. No notifications. New post. Michael O'Leary speaks to TCD Enterprise Society.

They wouldn't miss me here if I died: I haven't got involved in enough societies. You'd get that email from the staff that always goes around when there's a death.

Subject: Death of a Student

Dear Students and Staff,
We sadly inform you of the death of a student. Ellie Murphy, a third-year student in English Studies, passed away last week. Ellie was a promising Junior Sophister who planned to become a journalist after college.

They'd be nice about me sure. Because they wouldn't know that I won't ever make it as a journalist. They'd give me the benefit of the doubt. Don't speak ill of the dead and all that. If I kicked the bucket, they'd be lovely. They'd say:

If you are experiencing mental health issues, please contact...

And so on. They follow a formula, right? The emails for when staff and students die, I mean. There must be guidelines. They never say suicide, sure. Killed, by her own hand. Took the easy way out. Topped herself. There's no nice word for it. But then it's not a nice thing, so why would there be a nice way to say it?

Almost two years since Jack killed himself. I remember the apartment in halls when I found out. I was sitting at the kitchen table. Saw it on Facebook and I literally couldn't believe he was gone. Sounds like a cliché, that – 'literally couldn't believe it' It was so bloody horrible, and I can't even think of an interesting way to express it. But it's true: I couldn't believe it. I stared at my screen for five minutes straight. Didn't think. Stared so long I could see each pixel on the page floating there. I said 'WHAT?' out loud and I meant it. There was no food in the apartment. I had to wipe off my tears and go over to Jessie's to ask if I could have some beans on toast. I hadn't even spoken to Jack properly since fifth year, barely knew him anymore.

Last time I saw him, a few months before college, he was walking with his parents on Killiney Hill. I was out with Dad because it was sunny, and I saw a figure in a Jack Wills tracksuit at the crest of the hill. I thought: that's Jack.

He didn't see me. If I'd walked past him on the path, I would've said hi. I wouldn't have told him I always thought that he was kind, because I wouldn't have needed to. Maybe my dad would've said something to his dad. South Dublin dad chat. It would've been a bit awkward and then we would've been away. And that would've been nice.

Me and Dad walked on, he disappeared over the hill, and then he went away into eternity. A silhouette in the distance, a heartbeat of recognition, a thought of saying hello – that's all you get. That's all I got.

Because everyone knows someone, don't they? There was a girl in my sister's year, at the Protestant school. Eve something? Or was it a different school? So pretty in the photo, so happy and peaceful. She seemed so lovely. All that stuff whirring around her head, and all she seemed was lovely.

Ciaran said something about one of his friends. Walking back to his, the night we slept together, he said:

'This is the pub my dad took my pal and myself to after Limerick were in the All-Ireland.'

And I said:

'Is your friend in college?'

He said:

'No. He's not around anymore. He—'

Then he looked away. He had the same look on his face when I called him a culchie: frowning, but turning his face away so I couldn't see it. Like he didn't want me to see him feeling.

I wish I hadn't bloody said it. But he changed the subject right away. He was kind of like that during sex – as if he wanted to say something, not something bad, just something. But he couldn't. Or maybe I'm imagining it.

He was kind really, but he didn't like me. He didn't like my humour, obviously.

A crash in the atrium. I jerk up and peer down towards it. A girl with pigtails and a raincoat leans over frantically at the far end of the room. Bends her back to pick up what fell: a laptop. Around the atrium, eyes are fixed upon her. She turns around with the laptop in her hand and says nothing – she knows she's being looked at. She's almost performing, putting the laptop into the charger, showing everyone it's okay. Nothing to see here. I sit down before she can see me looking.

A week ago, some lad spilt some Club Orange up here. He didn't get the cleaners – too embarrassed probably – just some paper towels. The floor was sticky and sweet-smelling until the next morning. It made him look worse, clearing it up by himself, nobody helping him out or making a joke about it.

I felt sorry for him because you know people would talk. They would never say anything, but they'd talk. Straight onto the group chats. 'Jesus, did you see the lad who spilt his Club Orange everywhere?' But they'd never say it. That's what this university is: a place where everyone talks, but no-one makes a sound.

Instagram. Three new posts. One is Bill Withers. One is a girl from college on holiday in America. Caption: an American flag and 'Sunshine'. One is from Amnesty International, about a child killed in Sudan. She looks gorgeous. The girl from college, I mean. Hair back, sunglasses resting on her hair, pretty pearly smile. I like it .

I look up. It's so dark outside now; what little light there is can barely get into the library. At this time, the concrete doesn't so much turn a darker shade of grey as a dimmer one. It fails to reflect the lamps and you almost have to squint to see there's pillars and walls, not just holograms.

God, that girl is gorgeous. I look away from Instagram and catch my face in the mirror made by my sleeping laptop screen. I'm frowning without meaning to. My hair's gone into drowned rat mode. I look like someone to avoid, that's how I look, to be honest. But then I'm badly lit. If I was well-lit, maybe I could be happy.

If I died, they'd probably have some dynamite stuff to say about me. Probably they'd do an exclusive family funeral and my friends would do remembrance drinks for more of a laugh. Somewhere in Killiney, not Wicklow. Couldn't drag people down there for that – it's depressing enough already.

I'd have to write a note. I wouldn't want them to feel bad about it, but I'd want to leave something to the world. It would have to be well-constructed.

I'm sorry to burden you but—

No.

I'm sorry to put this burden on you but—

Better.

I don't feel like I can go on living like this.

No. That's such a cliché.

I'd have to create something that would fit with it all. The window closed, the door half-open, the house eerily silent. Dim light falling on my desk. The little envelope resting there, waiting to be discovered: *'To My Parents'*. The spectacle of it. The drama.

A gust of wind smashes into the library's walls, screeching as it hits. It's loud enough that some people in the atrium stop their work and look around the room with wide eyes, startled. Then the rush dies down and a calm, constant call replaces it once again. The wind settling into uneasy action.

But there's no such thing as a good suicide note. Even Kurt Cobain, Virginia Woolf: they're barely coherent. They're just lost – nothing else. What Jack did to his family. What he did to all of us. If he'd just…

But he was never that expressive. He never plucked up the courage, at the party, even though were both plastered. To kiss me, I mean.

We left the house and we were out in the garden for ages, listening to the music humming far away. Talking for so long I started to sober up and come back to earth. He kept trying to talk deep, but he couldn't do it: he couldn't express himself. We got down to the end of the garden, behind the hedge, and he said:

'There won't be a night like this again,' looking wistfully at the hedge.

And I laughed – not because he was wrong: he was right – but because I felt so giddy just to be there. He looked like the lead in a high school movie, casting his gaze romantically like that. And I took the piss out of him a bit, and then we talked a bit more. And it was funny. But he came back to it eventually.

'It's a beautiful night,' he said.

And so it was. It was one of those bright midsummer nights where it never gets dark until it's too late to care. One of those nights that only come around when you're sixteen. I was only wearing a crop top and a skirt, but I didn't feel a chill at all. It was the drink sure, but there was more to it than that. He was standing close to me, and in the dying heat I swear I could feel the warmth of his heart pumping blood. The wind picked up then, but it didn't matter. It felt so real, so alive – it was impossible to be cold. We were warm together.

'Yeah, it is,' I said.

'Yeah.'

He must have been telling himself to say that and then make the move, because he was painfully silent for a few seconds before he said it:

'You're really pretty.'

He looked me square in the face. I was stunned still, no idea what to say. My heart was beating into oblivion as my breath quickened and my eyes met his. They were dark, nearly the colour of the night behind them, but the whites were wide and widening as he locked onto me. I thought that he was going to kiss me right then, but he waited, and waited, and waited, and then—nothing.

Maybe if I'd stopped thinking and just kissed him. But I didn't have that kind of confidence. It's so hard to just do what you want to do. We looked at each other, and we waited, and we did nothing—and then he broke eye contact. It was him, not me. I'm sure we would've kissed if he'd just looked at me another two seconds. One of us would've got the message.

But it couldn't have happened like that, because it didn't happen like that. I heard he shifted another girl a couple of weeks later, and I shifted another boy the next time we were at a party together. And that was that. I never expected anything to come of it, and it didn't. Nothing came of it. Nothing could've been different.

Laughter. Two boys are messing around at the top of the stairs. It's the beautiful boy in the beige jacket again. He's with a friend whose back is turned to me. His friend feints a punch at him and he flinches, then they both burst out laughing louder than they should in a library. He floats his shoulders left and right in a boxer's stance as he grins and says:

'Right, sound, see ye this weekend then.'

He hears the same from his friend and then he's away, pitter patter down the stairs and out of view. His friend walks towards my desk, smiling as he passes. I smile back and watch him walk away from me. Then he's just pitter patter as well.

Everyone's filtering out of the library now. I close my eyes for a second, hearing but not seeing footsteps as they tap down the stairs. There's voices everywhere, chatting and laughing as they get ready to end the day. I take a moment to appreciate what's around me. Unsteady silence, broken constantly by footsteps, the tapping of keyboards, and the wind breaking against the building. And the rain too, coming down hard, giving us all it can. The library is full of these little noises. It's alive – all of it. All of us – we're alive.

I shut down my laptop and pack it away, throwing my phone into my bag. I skip past everyone who's studying late and then down the stairs, towards the wind and the rain. A can cracks open: the smell of Red Bull seeps into the air. I get to the exit and step into the storm.

I'm there a moment alone in the square as the wind shakes the trees to their roots and the raindrops fall like bombs. That's it: it rains, it rains every single day. On Jack, on me, on everybody. I look into the storm and smile.

Let it throw everything it can at me. Let it do its worst.

Lockdown 3000 in Future Dublin

I watch the white man raise his gun to the head and shoot the head. The eyes go blank in a second and then the head droops down without control. The white man says something in a European language which I do not understand then points at the camera as if he is showing off to me. This violates several graphic violence guidelines and there is no way I can allow it to be posted on The Network.

So I ban it.

I cite celebration of violence, but there are many other guidelines that I could mention. I am sure that my supervisors at The Network will agree. Therefore my Accuracy Rating will improve and, if I keep up the good work, I may be selected for Vacation when they lift restrictions again.

Now I must view more flagged content. Then I will take my Wellness Break.

***

One of these is a video of an Indian teenager punching another boy until he no longer resists. The second is a dog being shot. The third blames the Jews for the new pandemic. It says that the new virus was manufactured in an Israeli university for the containment of the Arab population, which is growing. I swipe left on the content, which bans it.

It's time for my Wellness Break. I close my browser and select the Grieving app, which I have recently downloaded. My device projects a hologram of my mother into the air and she floats around, bluish-coloured, wearing a female business suit which I have selected as her outfit. There were no Bengali-style clothes available, and I always imagined that my mother would wear this kind of suit once she became successful in Ireland.

'It is fantastic to see you, Salman!' she says in English, 'I'm so proud that my son is a Junior Content Moderator at The Network! The Network is all about bringing people together, and by being together we will all get through this difficult time! I notice that you have only spent seventeen minutes on the Dating app this week. Surely you should purchase the premium version to unlock the app's best features! Remember that Premium Users go on twice as many dates! By unlocking Dating Premium, you also unlock Grieving Premium at 40% off! Then you will enjoy Grieving ad-free…'

I am used to adverts.

'… and enjoy additional relatives at no extra cost!'

I have no other relatives.

She looks down on me with deep brown eyes which are beautifully rendered.

'Now, Salman. How would you like to grieve today?'

She looks more European than she should. Also, she never spoke to me in English, even after we came to Ireland. But the Bengali-language setting is littered with grammatical errors.

***

We are allowed to work from home during lockdowns as long as we sign two legal waivers. It is a privilege to have the choice and I work well from my bed since my last roommate was evicted.

The rest of my shift is easy. There is violent pornography and a nude photo of the President which is impressively realistic. After this I clock out and take my allotted exercise.

My mother could never get used to the wind in this country. On Gardiner Street, a bitter gust blows packets of Tayto Crisps at me and I trip to avoid them. A car rushes past and in the window I catch a glimpse of a shadow of a face. A few legs cross the street as rain splatters off their umbrellas, but there is nobody else. Perhaps people are afraid of the new virus, but usually the weather is more important.

As I walk back in the rain, I hear a girl singing from the council flats opposite my house. It comes through a microphone and it is too distorted, or the accent too strong, for me to understand. Still it is something alive and it stops me for a minute as I turn my key in the door. Somehow I hear in it the sound of my mother's lullabies.

Five minutes later I am alone in my room and the live voice has given way to pop music which demands that I have a good time.

***

I have completed today's Moderation Quota, but still I feel I can do more. Always you can work harder. Always there is work to do. The rain outside grows louder and I start tomorrow's Moderation Quota. This is how I will get selected for Vacation.

Unfortunately odd things happen in the next hour.

First, I must view some flagged Hate Speech. This is difficult because The Network finds many things hateful which I do not, for example copyright infringement. Also, much content that I find hateful is not found hateful by The Network.

My supervisor has sent me one such piece of content, which he says I have banned incorrectly. The caption states that the Muslims are outbreeding the Irish in this country and that there will be no Irish left in thirty years except half-breeds. My supervisor comments that this does not violate any guidelines and that I should not let my political opinions influence my work. I feel weak as my Accuracy Rating falls to 76%.

Outside the rain gushes into the gutters the colour of blood. It is the dead leaves again. If this keeps up the tap water will become undrinkable.

The next piece of content is also unsatisfactory. It should be the simple matter of a beheading. The thumbnail shows the classic kneeling figure surrounded by antagonists. His face is full of fear except for the bottom half which is covered by a large red play icon. I press play.

The video is a blend of sand, skin, and pixels. The kneeling figure is surrounded by men, one of whom carries a sword as he paces around kicking up sand. The kneeling man says something, pleading for his life, and a leg whirs into his stomach in response. He gets back to his knees and raises his hands in supplication. A glook of spit smacks into his face.

His hands lose focus as they tremble. Through the grain I see tears rolling down his cheeks as he moans for them to stop, his voice getting weaker and weaker with each plea. Everyone steps back except the man with the sword, who raises the shimmering blade and shouts.

It is clear that this man will die. I should shut the video off now, ban it, forget about it, but in this split-second something stops me which I cannot understand. I do not ban it.

I do not.

Now the kneeling man turns to face me. The rest of the picture freezes. All the other men look like they are on a green screen that has been paused, even though before it was grainy and mobile and could not possibly have been filmed with a green screen. They all look computer-generated, uncanny and flat and unreal. Only the kneeling man has three dimensions. His eyes seem to spasm as they fill with terror.

He looks at me, at me alone.

'Salman!' he cries, 'Salman!' Our eyes meet. 'Help me! You can help me!'

I fumble the device away from me, shrieking as his eyes lock on to me full of fury and agony.

'Salman!' he screams, 'listen to me!'

'You're not here! I can't do anything!' I scream back.

In a millisecond I scramble for the pause button. Now he is covered by the large red play icon, with only his terrified eyes still visible. In a frenzy I swipe left and ban the content and then it is gone and I am safe and I can begin to breathe again.

The night that follows I toss myself around the bedsheets. There is no rhythm to it, only spasms of random electricity.

The alarm on my device awakes me with notifications from Grieving. The app opens automatically and my mother's hologram rushes out to meet me.

'Good morning, Salman,' she says in English, 'I am so proud of you for meeting your Moderation Quota yesterday. I notice though that you have not updated your Dating profile for one hundred and thirteen days. Perhaps you should upgrade to Dating Premium, which also entitles you to 50% off Grieving Premium!'

I tell her that the content has started to talk to me. I ask her whether it is possible that the kneeling man was truly seeking me out or whether I am simply losing my grip on reality. I ask her to please help me.

Her hologram freezes in the air for several seconds, translucent and tinged blue as she sends my information off to the database. Then she looks down on me with tender eyes and flawless skin and asks have I considered downloading the Mindfulness app?

***

Dublin is grey and brown as I walk to the office.

Always here is the wind. After we landed at Dublin Airport, my mother and I stood in the chattering wind for two hours as we awaited Processing. I opened up my coat and snuggled her into it to try to keep her warm. It was when she did not stop shivering that I understood how she would struggle in this country and this weather. Now my cheeks burn numb in it and I put my hood up. The grey, the brown, the wind. Always here is the wind. Still, we had no choice but to come here.

And as we stood on the runway the mountains loomed over us and the men in hi-vis jackets told us to have our documents ready.

This morning my thoughts are full of these memories. I pass by the queue outside the supermarket on Parnell Street as a woman moans into her device. She says that they will never lift restrictions now that they know they can control us.

This I find very generic. They will lift them but then they will come back and then they will lift them and so on. I have heard this all so many times that I would rather listen to the mechanical drills of the builders and let my memories swim through my mind.

***

The office is a string of disconnected corridors with no discernible pattern. I hope to talk to somebody but no one is in. This is lucky though because it means I get my own workpod, a tiny room with flickered paint and a light without a lampshade. I sit on a white chair, clock onto my device, and several hours pass.

The work is mostly pornography, which I can ban more-or-less on the sight of an exposed breast. I am sure that my Accuracy Rating is soaring and I may be selected for Vacation after all.

Then there is a field in which stands a pretty, pale girl. It is bright green and birdsong twitters at the back of the picture. To the girls' left are pine trees and behind her stretches an infinite flowery meadow.

She stands here surrounded by life. Then she speaks calmly as the sunshine fills the sky. The language I do not understand but it is soothing and my lips curl up into a smile. I feel myself under a spell. Her lips get closer in the picture. All I can hear is her beautiful voice and the chirping birds nearby. Still her lips get closer.

Then her lull curdles into a repulsive scream and her tonsils rip back and forth in her throat. The picture pans out to men with balaclavas who surround her from thin air. They stop and slap and kick her and rip her clothes and her scream pierces my bones. Suddenly I see no meadow, only a close up of her tonsils screaming in glorious high definition as hands and fingers and other body parts writhe around her lips.

Again it is like all else is computer-generated and only her suffering is real. She looks at my eyes and shrieks

'Salman! Salman!'

And then in English she says 'Salman, help me! Help me! They are killing me! You have to help me, Salman!'

My chair crashes into the floor as I stand up and put my face millimetres from the screen, howling

'How?! How?!'

But she says only

'Salman! Oh please, God, please Salman! Please help!'

'I CAN'T,' I shout, 'I CAN'T HELP ANYONE! DON'T YOU SEE? IT'S NOT FAIR FOR YOU TO ASK ME THIS!'

'Please help!' she screams, 'Salman!'

'BUT WHAT CAN I DO?'

And as her scream reaches a nauseating crescendo I ban the video. My device tells me that sixteen minutes have passed, then I look away from it to pick my chair off the floor. I tell myself that I am in a small room in Dublin. I try to believe it. Eleven minutes later I receive an instant message from my supervisors. They tell me that devices have picked up suspicious sounds from my workpod. Is there a problem?

I reply that I heard no suspicious sounds at all and that there is no problem.

I take my Wellness Break but even after my fifteen minutes are up I still want to cry. Therefore I stay in the disabled bathroom for the rest of my shift and do no more moderation. I do this even though my Accuracy Rating will certainly slide and I may be placed on unpaid Wellness Leave.

***

That night the girl returns. I lie on my back on the green grass as she looks into my eyes and climbs on top of me. She doesn't say anything but only smiles softly as my fingers touch the flowers growing beside us. I have nothing to do but relax as we move with each other rhythmically.

In the next moment she transforms into a hag, cackling maniacally as she slashes at my neck with long sharp claws. She tears into my neck and rips out a chunk with her fangs. As her hot breath fills my mouth, I see her face has no features apart from bloody eyeballs. The rest is just pixels, 240p or less. I cannot breathe.

As my air runs out, she tells me that this is all a gift. Now I can feel pain again. Now I can help.

I know I am awake so there is nothing to wake from. Still I sincerely wish to return to whatever is left of the real world, to my room and to the light. After some seconds I am back, gasping for air and snatching the light switch.

When daylight finally comes my device tells me that my Accuracy Rating has plummeted and my supervisors are concerned. Also data analytics show that I have only used the Grieving app for thirty-five minutes this week. The app opens without me selecting it and my mother fizzes out in her holographic shade of blue.

'Good morning, my darling,' she says, 'you are spending less time with me. Would you like to change my outfit free of charge? Would you like to change my Key Grieving Phrases? Your feedback makes Grieving better for everyone!'

I swipe left but she doesn't go away.

'It is fantastic to see you, Salman! I think it's a great idea to check in with Qualified Wellness Therapists every now and then, don't you? After what you told me yesterday, I reported you to The Network. They have arranged a Wellness Session for you today at 15:30 at 616A Talbot Street. This will be provided free of charge and will take place in a special Wellness Room designed to promote mindfulness. Also, your position as a Junior Content Moderator is under review. Have a beautiful session!'

Her smile twinkles as it never twinkled in life.

'And a fabulous day!'

***

The Wellness Room is made up of four white walls with a single black chair under the shadow of a giant TV. In the corner, there is an LED waterfall with a plastic garden at its foot.

There is a moment of silence as I sit down on the chair and then the therapist flashes up on the TV. She is a low-res face with mousy hair, glasses, and pointless grey eyes. I force a smile out of my lips but she does not respond with any emotion which I can register. Then she is flicking through her notes.

'Have you been suffering from bad dreams?' she asks.

'I am not sure.'

'Your data says that you've been suffering from hallucinations.'

'How do you know that?'

Her face screws up as if I have insulted her.

'It's what your data says.'

'I don't know if I have been suffering from hallucinations. It is true that I see bad things, but that is part of my job.'

'Are these hallucinations or are they just content?'

'I don't... how can I tell the difference?'

'One happens in your mind and the other happens... well, it happens somewhere else. One is real and the other isn't.'

'And which is which?'

'That should be obvious.'

'But there is no difference at all. Do you understand? There is no difference.'

She looks at me blankly then says

'I can prescribe you something for this.'

I want to tell her that she is wrong. These people are not hallucinations.

This lockdown. This device. This city. These are my hallucinations.

Instead I ask her whether I might still be selected for Vacation. She tells me that this will not be possible until at least next year. Even if she wanted to, she doesn't have the authority to override the algorithm.

***

After I have paid for my prescription, I walk south from Talbot Street and cross the Liffey. From there I walk along the quays through the grey paths towards the Poolbeg Lighthouse. Between it and me is a thin stretch of sea wall unsheltered from the wind. It would look like it reached into infinity if I couldn't see that red lighthouse at the end. Behind me industrial chimneys fade into the darkening sky.

I walk along the sea wall as the waves spit foam up and the wind blows stronger. I remember being carried over this sea when we first came to Ireland, peering out the plane window at the land below, the mishmash of grey and green and concrete and grass and the Poolbeg Lighthouse the only red I could see in all of Ireland.

A year and a half later my mother lay in hospital holding my hand and clinging to an oxygen mask. She told me that she loved me, then when she could no longer talk her eyes told me it without words. After she died, I walked out of the hospital into this wind and realised that there was nobody I loved left in the world. This same wind.

Now it numbs my cheeks and sends me into a little shiver. I have reached the lighthouse.

I stare out to the ocean and it stares back at me formless and infinite. Imagine I jumped in and let myself roll with the waves, or swam through their foamy hair until I couldn't swim any more. The waves sweep a stone off the rocks and wash it into oblivion.

They break against the wall. Then pull back. Then break again.

Suddenly it comes to me. Somebody is suffering somewhere. Their pain is mine too. I am not alone. I am never alone.

It means something. It means something. It means something.

I'm Sorry, Girl

I'm sorry girl, I get
scatty sometimes. I hope
you don't judge me for it,
but I know you do. That's
fine.

I won't hold it
against you, when I hold you,
which I will, soon.
That's when I'll tell you
something clean
that makes you
clean, and it'll take
the scatty
right out of me.

And then we'll both grin
and be all clean together;
and your picture will make me
a perfect mirror.

Essays

The Snip

When you get circumcised in the UK, they send your foreskin to the lab for 'analysis'. After that, it goes to landfill.

I'm not sure why it needs to be analysed — what they think they'll find — but that's what the surgeon told me when I asked, after the operation. I wasn't brave enough to ask if I could keep it. If the fentanyl I was coming down from had been stronger, maybe I would have.

About 1/3 of men on Planet Earth are circumcised, most of them as babies. It's much harder to persuade a semi-rational adult to get rid of his foreskin, which is probably why most religions make sure to do it while boys are totally helpless.

Many famous pe–, I mean, people have undergone the procedure after infancy. With mixed results, it has to be said. At the turn of the 20th Century, circumcision was thought to prevent masturbation; and it was for this reason that Dr J.H. Kellogg, of Corn Flakes fame, recommended it for boys without anaesthetic. He also recommended electricity to deter masturbation (Jesus Christ) and, for girls, the application of carbolic acid to the clitoris (Jesus fucking Christ).

Slightly more successful was the circumcision of John F. Kennedy. He was circumcised aged 21 (I was 22) and wrote to a friend afterwards that 'J.J. [the name of his penis — don't ask] has never been in better shape or doing better service.' Later, he said he thought of circumcision as a 'threat to manhood, so you have to go on proving "it" is okay by any means possible.' And no prizes for guessing what he meant by 'proving "it".'

Adult circumcision remains rare. It's a long road to the operating table: it took two years of flashing my dick at medical professionals before they agreed to get rid of it, and another year before they actually took me under the knife. I was asleep, by the way.

You can get it done on the NHS, if you're persuasive enough, but if you don't have a valid medical reason then you'll have to pay cash. Anyone who wants to become a pornstar, or a Jew, or both, will have to cough up. It turns out that there are some things the British taxpayer just won't foot the bill for.

***

Like everything in healthcare, it starts with a lot of waiting. You're told to come at three, so you do. Half an hour later a nurse sees you, takes your blood pressure, disappears, comes back, leaves again, then comes back to tell you the doctors will see you soon. So you wait again.

You spend an hour in the company of *Hello!* Magazine until your anaesthetists pay you a visit. The gist of their speech is a description of morphine fentanyl, the general anaesthetic which converts what would otherwise be horrific torture into a very specific kind of powernap. They're odd sorts in an odd profession — people who administer powerful opiates for a living. I wouldn't trust either of them with your drink.

Finally, your surgeon comes in and tells you to flash your dick at her. This is the last time you'll do this to a medical professional, so enjoy it. But not too much.

***

Now it's time for you to go under the knife. Before the procedure starts, though, you have to get your fentanyl, which your anaesthetists administer while making terrible small talk in an effort to distract you from the fact that you're about to get knocked the fuck out.

My anaesthetists made some of the most hideous small talk in human history. There were two of them — one male, one female — and they acted like a married couple waging civil war.

'Would you believe it, he's moved my tools again', she said, expecting me to offer an opinion, 'it's a wonder we don't kill anyone.'

I elected to take the silent response which I have always found advisable in the midst of other people's domestic bullshit.

'See, she's always complaining', he said.

She smiled at me then snarled at him. I strained to make myself look harmless and irrelevant, something like a baby penguin.

Then the small-talk began. It was horrific.

'Ah, you go to university in Ireland? Drinking a lot, eh?', he said to me, slipping a mask over my face as thoughtlessly as he slipped into Irish stereotypes.

The mask muffled my response, which was probably incoherent anyway, but he replied as if we'd truly connected.

'Haha, you're right, they drink a lot of Guinness.'

I never said anything about Guinness.

'Yeah, my cousins live in Dublin', said the woman.

'Where?' I asked.

She didn't answer, didn't even acknowledge the question. The relief washed over me in an awesome wave.

'I'm gonna slip this in now. You'll feel a little pinch', she said.

I did feel a pinch: the tube pushing through my wrists into the vein.

They kept talking but it felt like there was an elephant in the room. Namely, I was going to be unconscious in fifteen seconds. The last thing I heard was the man telling me I was about to feel something 'like five pints of Guinness.' The last thing I thought was that I'd be ready for a cheese toasty after five pints of Guinness, not a bloody circumcision.

***

Your first thought when you wake up from your circumcision is the same as everyone else's. 'Fuck! I want to look at it!' It's like getting a haircut.

Your second thought, though, is that your mum is sitting in the corner, smiling pleasantly and asking how you feel. So hold your horses.

You get your first peek when you pass urine, which you have to do before the doctors discharge you. That's when you notice the swelling. Now, it might be different for you, but I wasn't told there would be swelling (or, if I was, I wasn't listening). So when I saw my penis post-op, I thought I'd be stuck with what I saw for the rest of my life. Probably this was the consequence of my fentanyl semi-daze, from which I was still emerging.

It's not easy to describe how a circumcised penis looks post-op, and it's not pleasant either. But I'm going to go do it anyway.

Well, okay, it's swollen. Now you might think: swollen! great! a free penis enlargement! But it's not really swollen like that. It doesn't swell in length, see, but in girth. As in it gets very wide. Fat, so your penis doesn't look much like a pornstar's: it's more like a third testicle.

There's this famous story about St. Patrick explaining the Holy Trinity to a pagan Irish king. St. Patrick shows him a three-leafed shamrock: each leaf is individual, but it is also one third of an indivisible whole — just like the Father, the Son, and the Holy Spirit.

Well, extend this metaphor to the post-op cock and balls. Each part is individual, but they look and feel like a cohesive whole. This is what enters your mind as you take your first circumcised piss, which comes out like a jet.

***

Now you've pissed, you're allowed to go home. But there's some bad news too: you're not allowed to have sex for a month. This, ahem, won't actually be much of a problem.

So you go home with a delicious pack of codeine and a limp. You haven't eaten all day because of the painkillers, so have a big meal and consume it like an animal. You can take your bandages off when you're comfortable and your stitches will eventually dissolve.

Don't panic. I know someone who ripped his stitches out post-op, causing unimaginable pain until he was lucky enough to pass out. Don't do that. You need a few days to relax, sleep, and get used to the new situation. That's fine.

There are some things you have to get used to. One night, with the codeine failing to numb your soreness, you fall into an anxious half-sleep. That night you have vivid, strange sex dreams of a kind you didn't even have as a teenager. I found that mine were mystical and powerfully felt, but not accompanied by sounds and only loosely accompanied by images.

Luckily, they're not wet dreams. Unluckily, the erections you wake up with will be painful: extra blood stretching the stitches which hold you together. (You can imagine the ghost of J.H. Kellogg licking his lips at this pain).

But time is the greatest healer, and it will heal your broken penis much quicker than it heals a broken heart.

***

Now you are in recovery. This is a routine: it makes time nothing special, puts the future ahead of the now. There are no intense moments, no moments of elation. But there are slight improvements, over and over again. Your swelling goes down. You walk lighter. You settle back into life knowing that something about your body has irreversibly changed. But you'll have to wait to see whether this is good or bad.

There are setbacks. Two days after the operation, you visit a friend in the countryside and tell him about it. Trampling mud under limping legs, you're out in crisp air and enjoying the conversation. He's enjoying it too. You come to a tall gate and the climb is difficult for you, post-op as you are. With a grimace you clamber over and, safe on the other side, say that

'It does feel a bit like I've been—'

'Castrated?'

'I was going to say… cut. Not castrated.'

But do you feel castrated?

Sometimes, struggling to get into your pants because of the pain, maybe, yes. You worry that the pain which accompanies your erections will be permanent. Or, worse, that it will cause some kind of Pavlovian conditioning where you'll find sexual excitement uncomfortable — as if being raised Catholic wasn't enough.

***

This is an ideal time not to read conspiracy theories. It turns out that a lot of circumcised men blame their sexual problems on their parents, the Jews, and, occasionally, Hillary Clinton.

You can see the appeal here. Here in the West we're getting quite tense about the so-called Crisis of Masculinity, and a lot of men want to know why things have gotten a bit ropey. As usual Jewish people get blamed because, you know, unfortunately that's what happens to the Jews.

It doesn't add up, of course. Why would circumcision suddenly damage male health after thousands of years? Why would the Jews want us to be circumcised anyway? It's their special thing — like football for Brazilians or guilt for liberals.

It's a mark of our doomed civilisation that an age-old medical procedure can generate such controversy. There is something going on here which is much deeper than a medical debate. And this is where it gets sexy.

Because everyone feels like the best sex is happening somewhere else, right? In a survey a few years ago, about a third of male students in the UK reported that they'd had sex while at university — over half of all respondents had watched porn. People look for something to blame our sexual recession on, and circumcision is an easy target. It's a dog-whistle for all sorts of classic culprits: parents, Jews, doctors. Everyone who's usually blamed for fucking up our sex lives.

Conspiracy theories take a messy, complicated, but fundamental truth and then explain it in the most batshit way possible. QAnon piggy-backed on #MeToo, the paedophile scandals in the Catholic Church, and the fundamental truth that powerful people got away with rape for decades. It snowballed because Americans learnt to despise the celebrities who, in such a vacuous political culture, are the closest thing the country has to statesmen. Americans know that their elites are fundamentally false, they just don't know why. Wouldn't it be simpler if it was all because of a Paedophile Pizza Cult?

Radical Intactivists swim in the same waters. Male fertility is plummeting in the West. The birth rate is decreasing as well. For a considerable number of young males, pornography has completely taken over the function of sex. These are inarguable and distressing truths. Wouldn't it be easier if it was all the fault of feminists, or Jewish people, or circumcision, or anyone but ourselves?

***

It's normal to worry. But don't. The truth is that circumcision is a minor procedure and usually doesn't do that much. Trust me, I know.

And if you don't trust me, look at the scientific studies, which have mostly shown that there is no loss of sexual sensitivity after circumcision, nor are there long-term problems associated. That being said, I don't think I'd get my son circumcised. What's the point?

There are some benefits, but only if you're suffering from phimosis or at high risk of venereal disease. Some say it's easier to clean, but the difference is marginal at best. If a tight foreskin gives you pain, look into the snip. But don't expect to be sent to heaven or hell. If you were circumcised as a baby, I'm sorry to tell you that your sexual problems are probably caused by something else. Note that I assume you have sexual problems. Everyone over thirteen does.

***

A month and a half after the operation, you go on a first date with a girl from college. It goes well — so well that, after a few drinks, you go back to yours to sink some whiskey. As you both drink, you consider how to move from talking to kissing and, once that age-old conundrum has been solved, you move into a more serious state of affairs. Sex, that is.

That's when you realise that not much has actually changed. That sex is still a physical connection preceded by an emotional one. That your intimacy is reflected in your pleasure. And that, actually, what your penis looks like isn't very important — in case you needed reminding.

It might be a tragedy. It might be a triumph. But congratulations — you've recovered. A new world awaits.

How to Drink Well
for Cheap
(While Living in Dublin)

For God's sake, if you can afford to spend money on good alcohol, spend money on good alcohol.

When you are old and responsible, you will most likely find that you have a greater supply of good drink than when you were young, but less opportunity to enjoy it. You have kids, you have a job, you are tired, you are boring. Make no mistake: if you're in your twenties, you only have a decade to do binge drinking properly. So do.

This goes especially for those of you with rich daddies. Daddy himself probably appreciates a good Scotch — or pretends to — so he will prefer you to blow his money on good-quality poison. Despite the repeated assaults of the government, good drink is still one of Dublin's biggest strengths as a city.

Drink in a pub when you can. Try not to worry yourself too much about your pockets or your country's cultural alcoholism. Think like Flann O'Brien, not Leo Varadkar.

If you don't have money, though, you can have just as much fun. Maybe more. Probably slightly less. Just follow my advice.

The first rule is *do what the fuck you want*. There is nobody more insufferable than an alcohol snob. It's not an art exhibition and you're not an artist, even if you drink red wine.

Next, to some sad news: the second rule, which is this. *You might not be an alcohol snob, but everyone else is.* I'm afraid that if you drink something that doesn't conform people will judge you. Also, if you wear clothes, talk, or think in a way that doesn't conform, people will judge you. That's what people do. They're awful. That's the reason you're drinking in the first place, in case you forgot.

Now, with these rules in mind, feel free to ignore the advice which follows and call me a dickhead at your discretion.

Don't drink wine, especially if you're not drinking it with a meal. I'm sorry. There are plenty of good places to buy wine in Dublin but, in case you didn't know, they all cost thousands and thousands of euro. This is not just because wine is heavily taxed and imported, but because it is marginal to Irish drinking culture and always will be.

Drinking (cheap) wine in Dublin is like going to Rome and ordering McDonald's: it's fine, and you'll obviously do it anyway, but that doesn't make it a good idea. An exception to this is Buckfast. Buckfast is the paragon of cheap alcohol: rich, stimulating, and sweet. Liquid power.

What Buckfast isn't — in the Republic of Ireland, I mean — is cheap. In Dublin, Buckfast costs something like double what it costs in the North; in fact, it will cost you more than something that is actually wine. So if you want to drink it, come to a smuggling arrangement with your friend from Mid Ulster. There a bottle costs £2.50 and comes free with a sausage roll. Also, chase it with lager or the sugar will kill you. To be fair, it'll probably do that anyway.

Another thing to avoid is the cocktail bar. You're in Dublin, not Miami. The fact of the matter is that Mr Bartender is gonna make a shit cocktail menu because he's Irish and you're gonna order the worst thing on it because you're Irish too. Specifically, you will order something that costs at least €15, gives you the meanest measure of spirit imaginable, and is 99% sugar. Whippersnapper bartenders refer to these as 'Karen drinks', so watch out ladies — your inevitable Instagram picture isn't as stylish as you think.

That's not to say that cocktails should be avoided full stop. Just make your own. Most of the reason people avoid cocktails is because the recipes are cloaked in jargon, and because they're aggressively conformist. But let's unpack some of the jargon anyway.

'Simple syrup', which is everywhere in cocktail recipes, is just sugar dissolved in water 1:1. You almost certainly have the necessary ingredients lying around the house, and you can make a big batch which keeps for ages.

Bitters, liqueurs, syrups etc. are basically the mid-strength part of the cocktail that adds another layer of flavour. I concede that they are expensive, but they are usually the smaller part of the drink, so the bottle you buy will go further than you expect (if you can keep it from the semi-morons who will try to drink it straight). Also, there are plenty of good cocktails which don't really need bitters or don't need them at all. See Horse's Neck, Moscow Mule, and Tom Collins.

What is really indispensable for cocktails is fruit and ice. Most cocktails contain fruit juice or are garnished with fruit (most often lemon or orange) and, again, most of them require ice. This will not cost you very much at all, and you will only look like a bit of a dick walking around with orange peel hanging out of your drink. But, really, the host should be supplying these things.

Oh, if you're a host, I'm afraid I'm gonna have to burden you with a third rule. *Always have ice.* I'm sorry, but it's great for lukewarm white wine (I already told you to fuck off, snobs) and essential for cold mixed drinks. More than that, though, it is abominably cheap. In case you need reminding, it's water: according to the UN, literally a human right. So have it in the house.

Cocktails are all well and good, but I don't expect for a second that you will actually drink them. Which brings me to the important part of this. Cans.

Cans deserve to rank alongside Guinness and whiskey as an integral part of Dublin's drinking culture. If the tourist board really represented Ireland, posters of Pratsky and Karpackie and Druid's would be plastered all over Dublin Airport.

The beauty of can culture is that it's a leveller. Whether you're buying from an O'Briens (Southside), a Centra (Northside, usually), or even one of those strange off licenses where the man is never in the shop (by the Royal Canal), you'll get the same options.

It's patronising to tell you which to choose, but I'm going to do it anyway. One cider is okay, but after two or three your teeth will feel like Tangfastics. Leave it to the fourteen-year-olds on a trip to the Gaeltacht. Drink lager.

More expensive cans are obviously better, but some are better than others. Stella is decent. Heineken is good, but nothing like what you'll get in Holland. Carlsberg is bad. But really we should be going cheaper.

Don't drink Tesco Lager. You know how peasants used to drink low-strength beer to avoid dysentery? That's what Tesco Lager is. In a world of water filtration, it's unnecessary. See also, Dutch Gold — the only drink that gives you a hangover on the first sip. You should also be aware that the fella on the Dutch Gold logo (the one with glistening gold abs) is not an accurate reflection of your average Dutch Gold drinker.

The best cheap lager in Dublin is a toss-up between Karpackie and Pratsky. You can also get some passable (and strong) stuff in Eastern European shops for worryingly cheap, but you're probably not going to do that and I can't recommend it in good conscience.

Karpackie VS Pratsky is the great debate of our generation, sort of like what Fianna Fail VS Fine Gael was in the 1930s. Everyone knows they're basically the same, and everyone agrees they're pretty awful, but the debate over which is worse may well plunge the country into civil war. Pratsky is better.

I assume you know how to operate a ring pull, so I will keep patronising advice on consumption to a minimum, but bear this in mind. The freezer is your friend. If you have paper towels (let's face it — you probably don't) then put a wet one around your cans and whack them in there. If you don't have paper towels, let them stay in there naked for about half an hour and they'll probably be fine.

You don't need to be a scientific genius to realise that this is a risk, but it's a risk worth taking. Cold lager really is an entirely different drink to its lukewarm cousin. Ice-cold Pratsky, for example, is gorgeous; warm Pratsky should only be drunk by people in psychological turmoil. If you're considering warm lager, try religion first.

For a big night, a four-pack of cans should be paired with a spirit and mixer of your choice. Stay away from the naggins (200ml): they're overpriced and will be gone long before the night ends. A shoulder (350ml) will usually do, but on a real occasion go the full 750ml. Assuming someone steals from you — which they will — this is the only way to guarantee you'll have enough. On rare occasions, you'll even wake up in the morning with some left.

The best spirits to buy cheap are vodka and spiced rum. Spiced rum, I repeat: categorically *not* white rum, which is awful when cheap and not great when it's expensive either. The best cheap spiced rum is Captain Cook, Lidl's Captain Morgan rip-off which is arguably better than the real thing. The caramel notes are legendary.

Mix rum with juice, smoothie, or ginger beer. Coke is acceptable, especially since it will give you a little caffeine boost; but when it goes flat your drinks will become miserable. Ginger beer also mixes with vodka and lime to make the Moscow Mule and is one of the few drinks that mixes decently with whiskey.

Speaking of whiskey, this is one drink which I forbid you to go cheap on. Your ancestors didn't call it the water of life because they mistook it for Lucozade Sport.

Drink whiskey patriotically neat ('on the rocks' is the English way), with water, or, if you're not trying to impress anyone, with ginger beer. Bourbon mixes well, Irish mixes decently, and Scotch mixes awfully. Bear in mind also that whiskey brings alcohol snobs out like flies… so if you're ever told that it's genocidal to drink Jack Daniels & Coke, be sure to comfort the person in question. He has low self-esteem.

If you're feeling really cheap, don't be afraid of dilute/ squash. Vodka with orange squash and tap water sounds like a bad drink (because it is) but it's not all that different to a vodka and Club Orange/Fanta/whatever. The latter are just orange syrups mixed with carbonated water. I'm not saying I recommend the drink, but I probably wouldn't recommend what you're drinking at the moment either.

And, hey, the world's in a rough spot. It might be worth developing a drinking problem just to cope.

The Zombie Culture Wars

Imagine you're talking to someone at a party. But not this year. Go back a few years — let's say, to 2020.

You've had a few drinks and now, without you thinking about it, the chat has taken a left turn into controversy. It could be Black Lives Matter, it could be a Nike advert, it could be Jeremy Corbyn. In that year, it could really be anything.

Your companion starts really getting into it — they're waxing lyrical, they're setting the world to rights; you can tell they really *believe* this stuff. They're talking and talking, and now you start thinking...

Hold on, which side are they on?

You know what I mean. Pick an issue, especially one that was current around that time. Let's say vaccine mandates.

What would you think if someone said the government was trying to control people, or that vaccines were experimental, or that they wouldn't be taking the vaccine themselves? Would you listen impartially and reserve judgment? Or would you think: oh, hold on, *they're on that side.*

Let's look at it another way. What would you think if someone said the government wasn't doing enough to protect people, that unvaccinated people were dangerous, maybe even that the unvaccinated shouldn't be allowed into public places? Wouldn't you think: oh, *they're on that side.*

The point is that we've lived through an era where the big political and cultural debates pushed us into binary identities. Do you support lockdowns? Black Lives Matter? Trump? Brexit? #MeToo? These were not issues where it was easy to shrug your shoulders and wonder what Timothée Chalamet was up to. They demanded that you took a side, made a stand.

'Believe in something, even if it costs you everything', as Colin Kaepernick told us in a heartfelt and moving advert for sports equipment.

What did these binary identities achieve? For all their serious talk, what I remember about them is a lot of hashtagging and handwringing and shouting. We did all that, got really worked up, and then new horrors came along: Russia-Ukraine, Israel-Palestine, the Biden meltdown, and... where are we now? Who's on our team? Who are the bad guys again?

It turns out that pronouns and safe spaces don't lower inflation, just as Vladimir Putin is not a champion of family values. And the ethnic cleansing in Israel and Gaza —rough, I know... but Jesus, have you seen they're not delivering meals to Ivy League students on their camping holidays?

Now, it's obvious that debates about identity and culture are not going away — least of all for an English-born, Irish-educated writer with the pen name Sean Stones. I wasn't born in Ireland, I don't have the passport, and no matter how much I wanted to be Irish while I lived in Dublin, no one ever thought I was. So was I Irish-fishing when I wrote this stuff? Do you look at me in disgust if I spell my name Seán rather than Sean? Am I authentic enough for you?

And has Irish literature itself been inauthentic? Did it act like Ireland was all knitted jumpers and small towns and existential crises at a time when there were plenty of warning signs that violence against migrants was on the rise? Was it self-reflective and self-indulgent while its capital city drifted towards a race riot? Well, these are all culture war questions, and they're legitimate ones. The point is you can ask them without getting all sanctimonious about it.

As the Harvard professor Randall Kennedy wrote recently, this is a 'cultural struggle of long duration, one that has no end in sight.' And he'd know: his students must be insufferable. But he's right — no matter how many votes Trump or the Tory party get, these cultural dividers are not going away. Race, gender, climate change: they weren't just made up. But does anyone outside a hypercaffeinated group of activist losers (this goes for both sides) enjoy the way in which they've been talked about these last few years? Has taking them so seriously actually been helpful?

In 2024, the people who really *believe* in these culture wars — who want the cancellation and the handwringing apologies and the gross manipulation of language to go on — have no new ideas. They're not dead but, after years and years of breathless outrage, it's difficult to say they're alive. They moan and groan and stumble along like zombies, commanding our attention without saying anything fresh, consuming our brains with ideological air. They demand to be taken seriously. They are bad at telling jokes.

We don't need to be zombies. We can be conscious of identity without being defined by it. We can ask questions without expecting them to have an easy answer. We can laugh at woke people without becoming reactionaries, just as we can laugh at reactionaries without becoming snivelling ideologues.

The culture wars have caused a lot of drama these last few years; but... so?

Sean Stones was born in 1997 in Bristol, England. He moved
to Dublin in 2016 to attend Trinity College and lived there
until 2020. These stories were written during that time.

To find out more about Sean Stones' work, go to
pendulumpress.co.uk.

PENDULUM PRESS